Praise for

VICKI LEWIS THOMPSON

"Vicki Lewis Thompson is one of those
rare, gifted writers with the ability to touch
her readers' hearts and their funny bones."
—Debbie Macomber

"Ms. Thompson continues
to set the romance world on fire
and keep it burning."
—Diana Tidlund, *WritersUnlimited.com*

Award-winning author **Vicki Lewis Thompson** hangs her hat in Arizona, where the sun is hot and the chili peppers are even hotter. Her more than sixty sizzling romances fit right into the landscape. With more than fifteen million books in print worldwide, Vicki's earned both national and international recognition. Romance fanzines, *Romantic Times* and *Affaire de Coeur* have all honored her for her unique blend of spice and humor. The roof blew off her career in June 2003, when her first mainstream novel, *Nerd in Shining Armor*, became a Reading with Ripa Book Club pick and she hit all the major lists, including *New York Times* and *USA TODAY*. She's a seven-time finalist for Romance Writers of America's coveted RITA® Award. The mother of two grown children, she lives with her husband, to whom she's been married for an astonishing number of years, and a very spoiled tuxedo cat. Because desert living requires that she spend a great deal of time in the pool, she's waiting for someone to invent a waterproof laptop.

VICKI LEWIS THOMPSON

'Tis the Season

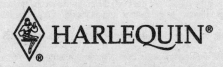

HARLEQUIN®

TORONTO • NEW YORK • LONDON
AMSTERDAM • PARIS • SYDNEY • HAMBURG
STOCKHOLM • ATHENS • TOKYO • MILAN • MADRID
PRAGUE • WARSAW • BUDAPEST • AUCKLAND

To my Aunt Bet and Uncle Ken Bradley,
Who cultivate awareness, friendship,
compassion...and Christmas trees

Special thanks, as well,
to the University of Connecticut
Cooperative Extension Service

ISBN 0-373-81076-8

'TIS THE SEASON

Copyright © 1989 by Vicki Lewis Thompson.

www.eHarlequin.com

Printed in U.S.A.

ANNA PLACED HER SACK of ripe tomatoes on the counter of the Sumersbury grocery and reached into her shoulder bag for her wallet. Before the balding man behind the cash register could ring up her purchase, a large woman barreled into the grocery and headed for the counter.

"Edward!" panted the woman. "Have you heard the news about Sammy?"

The man blinked and smiled apologetically at Anna before answering the woman. "No, can't say I have, Estelle." He pushed the keys on the old metal register and quietly gave Anna her total.

"Well, you must be the last person to hear." The woman smiled in triumph. "Sumersbury's going to be on national TV. *National* TV, Edward. Prime time."

"You don't say." Edward took Anna's money. "Why's that?"

"The TV people called Sammy an hour ago and told him they want to do a whole special about cutting the White House Christmas tree. They're calling it *A Connecticut Christmas*. Now what do you think of that?"

Anna glanced at the woman, who was built like a

hip-roofed barn. Anna hadn't met her before, but then she hadn't met most of the residents of Sumersbury. She'd deliberately kept to herself during her weekends at the farmhouse. But she had to ask about this television thing. Her peace and quiet could be in jeopardy if what she suspected turned out to be true. "Pardon me," she said, "but does this have anything to do with Garrison's Christmas Tree Farm?"

The woman turned to Anna. "It most certainly does. You must not live here, or you'd know that for sure."

"I only come up on weekends," Anna said, and instantly regretted offering the information.

"Oh." Estelle looked her over. Then she snapped her fingers. "You're the one! Daphne said some woman from New York bought the McCormick place as a vacation home."

Anna groaned inwardly. Now she'd done it. So much for keeping a low profile. "Yes, I'm the one," she said.

"So you're Sammy Garrison's neighbor. I can't believe you don't know he won that contest."

"I've never met Sammy—uh, Mr. Garrison," she said weakly. The news was getting worse and worse, but Anna decided to find out what she could. "What contest are you talking about?"

"Why, the annual Christmas Tree Growers' Association contest. Our Sammy took the grand prize this year, and one of his trees will be sitting smack-dab in the middle of the White House at Christmastime. Isn't that thrilling?"

"Thrilling," Anna said.

"And now this television special." Estelle's eyes gleamed. "I've already told Sammy that my ladies, the Sumersbury Craft Guild, will redo his house for him. Typical bachelor—no decorating sense whatsoever. We can't have the cameras filming the inside of Sammy's house the way it is, can we, Edward?" She turned for support to the grocer.

"I guess not, Estelle," the grocer said with a furtive glance at Anna.

"Well, I have to pick up a few things for dinner, and I have a million calls to make," the woman said, moving away from the counter. "Nice to have met you, Miss... What did you say your name was?"

"Tilford," Anna said, picking up her tomatoes with a resigned sigh. "Anna Tilford."

"I'm Estelle Terwiliger, dear."

Anna recognized that she was supposed to be impressed by the name, and she smiled vaguely. "Nice to meet you, too," she said. Her long, peaceful summer was over.

On the drive to her weekend home, Anna considered what she'd learned, and the irony made her laugh. Of all the secluded farmhouses in the state of Connecticut, she'd bought the one next to a place soon to be featured on national TV. She'd foolishly imagined that being situated between a Christmas tree farm and a wildlife preserve would give her the perfect setting to heal and regroup.

She'd further congratulated herself when someone on the Christmas tree farm unknowingly provided summer evening concerts on the harmonica. The plaintive sounds, distant and sweet, had filled her with comfort. The past couple of weekends, though, the harmonica player had been silent, probably because he was off winning Christmas tree contests and wreaking havoc with her country retreat. Great.

She pulled into her driveway and stopped, blocked by the red maple that had fallen early in the summer. The tree had toppled over during a midweek storm, so at least Anna's compact Ford hadn't been trapped inside the garage. But the barrier had forced her to lug her small suitcase and sack of groceries around the splintered trunk each weekend.

As she opened the car door, she heard a chain saw buzz from the direction of the Christmas tree farm. Already her quiet ambience was gone. She got out of the car and pushed the front seat forward to reach her suitcase in the back. Then she hefted the bag of nonperishables, put the sack of tomatoes on top and closed the car door with her hip.

The chain saw continued to whine in the distance as she carted her belongings around the fallen tree. Machinery like that could clear her driveway in no time, Anna thought, pausing on the brink of an idea. If Sam Garrison had a saw already in operation, surely he wouldn't charge her much to cut up one red maple. Besides, he'd entered a contest that might soon destroy her privacy. He owed her one.

After depositing her suitcase in the hall and her tomatoes and a partially thawed chicken in the refrigerator, she locked the front door and hurried back to the car. The chain saw still whined its noisy tune, but she had to be quick. The operator might stop any minute for supper, and the immediate opportunity would disappear.

Anna backed her car out of the driveway and caught a glimpse of herself in the rearview mirror. Wild woman, she thought, and chuckled. Her neighbor wouldn't be swept away with admiration for her baggy yellow sweats and her hair hanging in unruly corkscrews down her back. When she was a kid, her older brother, Jim, had said her hair reminded him of an orange sweater the dog unraveled. He'd also complained that redheads were supposed to have blue eyes, and her brown ones were the wrong color.

When Jim had gained some maturity, he'd apologized and said she was pretty, but Eric had been the first man to call her beautiful. He'd announced, with his artist's gift for hyperbole, that her hair reminded him of cirrus clouds at sunset and her eyes of rich milk chocolate. After they'd become lovers, he'd encouraged her to let her hair grow until it reached past the middle of her back. Then last year, when the fights had started, he'd minimized her anger by ascribing it to the color of her hair, thus neatly turning a former asset into a liability.

As she retraced her route along the lane that led past Garrison's Christmas Tree Farm and her house, Anna gazed at the low rock walls that bordered the lane and divided up the gentle countryside. She remembered Robert Frost's line from "Mending Wall" about good fences making good neighbors. Maybe in Frost's day they had, she thought, but these fences weren't high enough to shield her from TV crews and nosy townspeople.

She turned down the unpaved graded road that led to the white, two-story farmhouse. To the right of the house stood a red tractor barn, and the sound of the chain saw came from somewhere behind it.

Only a pickup truck, its green and white paint marred with rusty scratches, sat in the driveway area between the house and the barn, and Anna parked her car beside it. She got out and glanced past the barn to the precise rows of evergreens about two or three feet high. Baby Christmas trees, she thought, breathing in the freshness of pine. If it weren't for this stupid contest Sam Garrison had won, she could be more appreciative of the sweet smell.

The September daylight thinned as the sun settled closer to the horizon, and Anna walked briskly toward the barn to find the operator of the chain saw. She rounded the corner and spied him turned partly away from her. He reminded her of a picture in a country-living magazine, with his red plaid shirt and faded jeans and his dark, collar-length hair. No doubt the TV crews would love filming a scene like this.

Before she could call out, he braced a section of log across twin sawhorses and sent the chain saw into action. Anna stuck her fingers in her ears. When he was finished, she moved across the clearing with a loud "Excuse me," and he swung around, pushing his goggles to the top of his dark hair to glance at her in surprise. *His hair is as untamed as mine,* she thought, pleased to find someone else with impossibly curly hair.

"Can I help you?" He switched off the chain saw and rested it on a stump before taking out his earplugs.

"My name's Anna Tilford. I live down the road." Anna felt less sure of her request than she had at first. The efficiency of his movements and the decisive set of his shoulders intimidated her. "Are you Sammy Garrison?"

A smile twitched at the corners of his mouth. "You must have been talking to Estelle."

"Why?"

"She's the only one around here who's allowed to call me Sammy."

"Oh." Anna flushed. "Sorry."

"No problem. Nice to meet you, Anna. You bought the McCormick place?"

"That's right." As her embarrassment faded, she studied him. He was about her age or a little older, maybe thirty-two or three. High cheekbones, jaw as square as a spade, plenty of laugh lines around clear blue eyes—a good face.

"So you're the city woman everybody's wondered about." He smiled.

"So it seems." Anna had imagined herself nearly invisible in this tiny community, and yet she'd been the talk of the town. "And I have a favor to ask."

"Sure. Name it."

Just like that he'd agreed to help her. She was taken aback. "I need a chain saw," she blurted.

He regarded her with a knowing grin. "I was wondering when the new owner of that house would get tired of a tree down in the driveway."

Anna laughed and shook her head. "Nothing goes unnoticed around Sumersbury, does it?"

"Not much."

"Incidentally, I'd be more than willing to pay whatever—" She paused as a frown creased his tanned brow. "Now I've insulted you. I only meant—"

"It's all right," he said, taking a step closer as if to smooth the moment. "I understand. You're from the city. But one of the values I treasure here is the neighborliness, so let me do you a favor in that spirit, okay?"

"I...I appreciate it." He was right, she thought. She wasn't used to country ways—the neighborliness or the accompanying tendency to mind other people's business.

"I've about finished here," he said, glancing at the lengths of wood scattered around the sawhorses. "Let's get your tree out of the way before dark." He picked up the chain saw and started toward the parking area beside the barn.

"We can take my car," Anna offered as they approached the two vehicles.

Sam glanced at her shiny blue compact. "I think not. I'm covered with sawdust, and the chain saw might leak gas."

"Oh." She watched as he swung the saw into the back of the pickup. She hadn't noticed the sawdust before, but now she could see little flecks in his dark hair and covering his plaid shirt and jeans. She didn't think he was deliberately drawing attention to his body, but his comment had that effect for her. Despite her irritation about the TV special, she found herself taking inventory of Sam Garrison and liking what she saw.

He pulled the goggles from their resting place on top of his head, and sawdust puffed from his hair. "Whew," he said, brushing a hand across his eyes. "It'll be good to jump into the shower after this."

Again she supposed his remark was innocently made, but Anna felt less than innocent as she pictured him showering. She glanced away. "I'll bet."

"Come on into the house while I get the keys to the truck. Then I'll follow you over there."

She did as he suggested, all the while admiring the unself-conscious ease he displayed with her, a perfect stranger. Country ways were different from city ways, certainly. During the workweek in New York, she concentrated on the intellectual side of life, but here she was confronted with physical realities. Perhaps that was why she was so aware of this man's body. She'd found him involved in a physical task, not a mental one, so her thoughts were perfectly logical.

He held the front door open for her. "Be warned these are bachelor quarters," he said. "Make yourself at home while I grab my keys and wallet." He bounded up the stairs, two at a time.

Estelle had been right about Sammy's—no, *Sam's*—house needing attention before the cameras arrived. Anna stood in the middle of a parlor whose promise hadn't been realized. Her interior designer's eye noticed beamed ceilings and an elegant wing-backed sofa piled with ledger books. The sofa's upholstery, an unfortunate green plaid, clashed with the braided rug in front of it.

Two vinyl-covered armchairs flanked a huge blackened fireplace complete with giant andirons. Anna knew now why Sam had been using his chain saw when she arrived. A fireplace this large ate lots of wood each winter, she guessed. The decorator in Anna longed to sweep the mantel clean of its burden of junk mail, a pair of scissors, a rock paperweight and a ball of twine.

She noticed several attractive end tables, one of which looked like a Duncan Phyfe, and three serviceable but unremarkable lamps. None of the room's furnishings mattered, however, once she caught sight of an object tucked away in a shadowed corner.

Although Anna couldn't imagine why, Sam Garrison owned a magnificent eight-harness floor loom.

She approached the loom and laid her hand on the dusty maple as pleasure-filled memories returned. After her introductory weaving class in college, she'd promised herself that someday she'd buy a loom like this one and create wonderful weavings. Someday had never arrived.

Hearing Sam's footsteps on the stairs, she turned, one hand still on the loom.

"Do you weave?" he asked, coming toward her.

"Once upon a time. I've always wished that I— well, anyway, this is a beautiful loom."

"My grandmother's," he said, seeming pleased with her interest. "I should sell it instead of letting it sit here gathering dust, but I like the darned thing for some reason."

"Why not learn to use it?" Anna suggested, touched by this evidence of sentimentality. "I've heard of a football player who took up needlepoint, and this is the same idea, a stress reducer. Of course, with a job like yours, you may not have much stress to reduce."

Sam laughed. "I think in the past few weeks I've latched on to my share. Maybe I'd better take up weaving, at least until the first part of December."

"I heard about that today."

He glanced at her. "You don't sound too excited about the prospect."

"I'm not. I bought my house as a quiet retreat."

"Sorry about that. If it makes you feel any better, I'm not looking forward to this television deal, either." He stuck his hands in the back pockets of his jeans. "Winning the contest was okay, but I had no idea that would happen. Damn, there's the phone. I was afraid of this. Excuse me a minute."

He left for the kitchen, and Anna could hear him explaining the television special to the caller. He sounded weary of the idea already, and her feelings shifted from irritation to sympathy. He didn't welcome the invasion of cameras any more than she did, and she liked him for it. He returned and sighed.

"After I won the contest, the phone rang off the hook. Now with news of the special leaking out, I have that to look forward to again."

"How did everyone find out so fast? Estelle Terwiliger said you got the phone call this afternoon."

"My phone's been on a party line for years, and I never got around to changing it. Doris McGillicuddy listens in all the time, and she feeds all her information to Estelle." He shrugged. "It doesn't really matter. I wouldn't have kept the secret long, anyway, even without Doris."

"I'm beginning to understand that."

The telephone rang again. "Come on, let's get out of here. Let it ring."

"Are you sure?"

"If we don't leave, we'll never get your tree sawed up. The sun is setting and we're losing daylight."

"Okay." Ignoring the ringing phone with difficulty, Anna walked out the front door Sam opened for her.

As she drove ahead of Sam's truck down the lane to her house, she remembered the harmonica music she'd enjoyed all summer. A warm feeling enfolded her at the thought that Sam might be her unseen musician. She wondered whether or not to ask him about it.

She parked her car on the edge of the driveway to allow him access with the truck. Now that the task was at hand, she considered what to do with the wood after it was cut. Etiquette probably dictated that she offer it to Sam, although she mustn't imply that the wood was payment of any kind. She hadn't realized that she'd have to be so careful of country neighbor sensibilities.

They had barely enough sunlight to finish the job. Anna stood by while Sam adjusted his goggles and put in earplugs. Then, with a wrench of his arm, he started the chain saw buzzing. While Anna leaned against the front bumper of his truck and watched, he sliced the large truck into several manageable pieces.

She'd rarely watched a man perform a job as macho as wielding a chain saw. Although she'd never allowed herself to equate physical strength with masculinity, she kept glancing at Sam's flexing muscles. When he turned the motor off, Anna surprised herself by asking him to dinner. Usually she wasn't the one to take the initiative.

"I'd love to," he said, pushing the goggles to the top of his head.

"Good. And would you...would you bring along your harmonica?" It seemed that one risk led to another.

He looked startled. "How did you—"

"I can hear you," she said, glad she'd guessed correctly. "You've been my evening entertainment all summer."

He reddened and his pale blue eyes were bright with embarrassment. "I find that hard to believe. You said you liked peace and quiet."

"Sam, it's been lovely," she said, completely dropping her usual caution. "You have no idea how your playing has added to the atmosphere. After you were finished, I always felt so relaxed, and I thought someday I should find out who has given me such pleasure and thank them. Now I can."

He still looked uncomfortable. "I had no idea someone could hear me."

"Will you bring it?"

"I've never played for anyone before."

"Of course you have. You've been playing for me all summer. You just didn't realize it. Please. After all you've done, removing this tree for me, I have no right to ask more of you, but I've missed my concerts recently, and I'd love to hear you play right on my own back porch."

He looked doubtful. "It probably won't sound as good up close."

"I'll take my chances. Please." She smiled. "As a neighborly gesture."

Sam laughed and shook his head. "Catch on quick, don't you? Okay, but don't say I didn't warn you. You'll probably send me and my harmonica packing in no time."

Anna glanced into his eyes and felt a familiar tug at her heart. He really appealed to her. "Not likely."

"I'll stack your wood before I go home and clean up," he said. "Where would you like it?"

"I thought maybe you'd want it, for your fireplace."

Sam looked at the chimney protruding from her shingled roof. "Don't you burn wood in yours?"

"Yes, I plan to, but—"

"Then I'll split this for you tomorrow or the next day. Where's your woodpile?"

"There are a few logs around back," she said, giving up on evening the score. "And thank you."

"No problem," he said, tossing the first hunk of tree trunk into the back of his truck as if it were a feather pillow.

She watched him load the big pieces and then helped with the smaller ones, despite his worry that she'd scratch her hands. Working beside him and sharing the task added to the growing attraction she felt.

"I'll drive around and unload this if you have stuff to do for dinner," he said.

Anna thought quickly. The chicken would take

close to an hour, and he was probably starving after all the outdoor exercise. "Good idea," she replied. "Come on over whenever you're ready, and don't forget the harmonica, okay?"

He chuckled and swung into the cab of the truck. "If you say so."

What a sweet country man, she thought as he drove around to the back of the house and she headed inside to start the chicken. Their interaction contrasted so sharply with her city life that she felt like a different person. She had the urge to play the sweet country girl and shed the sophistication that ten years in the city had given her.

From the kitchen window she watched him unloading the wood in the thickening twilight. She couldn't remember anticipating an evening with such pleasure in a long time. In the past year of living with Eric, the constant fights had spoiled their shared time together. The inevitable parting last spring had been a relief, although after he'd left, the apartment had echoed with his remembered presence. She'd gladly fled to the country each weekend to escape the memories.

When Sam finished unloading the wood, he glanced up at the lighted kitchen window and waved. She waved back. Then he hopped into his truck and headed down the driveway toward the lane.

Once the chicken had been herbed, spiced and popped into the oven, Anna took a quick shower herself, but her only available clothes were the sweat suits she'd brought for the weekend. It didn't matter, she thought. This was her country idyll. She put on a pale lavender sweat suit that was slightly newer than the canary-yellow one, applied some fresh makeup and brushed her hair.

Back downstairs she glanced at the square dining table, a secondhand purchase hastily made, and felt a twinge of professional shame. She'd made no effort to decorate this house, although her New York friends assumed she used her weekends to create a showplace, one that she would unveil with a flourish when it was done. Anna couldn't admit to them, and barely to herself, how little interior decoration interested her these days. Her job, once a joy, had become a way to pay the bills.

She'd found a rebellious pleasure in not decorating her country house, but now a guest was coming to dinner, and she wished that she'd at least bought a tablecloth and a couple of candlesticks. Finally she ran back upstairs for a flowered sheet and a long piece of ribbon. She tied the sheet in flounces around the perimeter of the table and made a centerpiece with a wooden bowl of McIntosh apples and green grapes. Remembering the white utility candles she kept in case the electricity went out, she hollowed out two apples and used them as candle holders.

When she stood back to gauge the effect, she felt a satisfaction that had been absent from her work for months, and all she'd done was sling a sheet over a table and pile some apples in a bowl. Eric would probably have laughed at her homemade efforts, but Eric wasn't here. She didn't have to worry about his judgment, and Sam didn't seem like the kind to judge.

Sam arrived at the back door soon after she'd completed the table setting. His hair was still slightly damp from the shower, and he smelled of shampoo and soap. When he took off his light jacket and hung it on a peg next to Anna's, she discovered that, like her, he'd changed color but not kind of clothes. His plaid shirt was blue instead of red, and his jeans looked slightly newer than the ones he'd worn to cut wood. Otherwise he was the same sweet country man who had chopped up her tree. His harmonica made a narrow bulge in the breast pocket of his shirt.

He'd also brought a bottle of wine. "I took a chance," he said, handing it to her, "on what you were serving and if you even like wine."

She held up the Chardonnay. "I'm serving chicken and this is perfect."

"Good." He glanced past her into the dining room and gave a low whistle of approval. "Did you do all this since I left?"

"Well, yes. You're my first guest, and I—I had fun making a table setting out of odds and ends."

"I'm impressed." He glanced at her speculatively. "Exactly what do you do in the city?"

"Considering how the house looks," she said, "I'm

ashamed to tell you. It's a case of the cobbler's children going barefoot, I guess."

"You're some sort of professional decorator, aren't you?"

"Afraid so. But this summer I just wanted to relax, so I haven't tackled anything in here yet."

"Hey, I understand." He leaned against the kitchen counter and gazed at her. "And considering that this is your vacation spot, I have no business thinking what I'm thinking."

"That's a leading statement, Sam. You might as well come out with the whole thing."

He sighed. "Okay, but feel free to tell me to jump in the lake."

"All right." She folded her arms and waited.

"Well, the television network expects my farmhouse to look like something out of a magazine, and you've seen firsthand that it doesn't. Estelle and some of the women in town have offered to decorate the house for Christmas, but the idea makes me nervous. Can you imagine five or six little old ladies running in and out, draping things here and there like fairy godmothers?" He glanced at her in pathetic appeal.

Anna laughed, picturing Estelle directing traffic in the middle of Sam's parlor. "So you'd like me to make a few decorating suggestions? I can do that." Fair was fair, she had to admit, and neighborliness worked both ways.

"More than a few suggestions, Anna. I'd like you to do the whole house, top to bottom."

So much for her country idyll, Anna thought. So much for evenings before the fire with her newfound friend, listening to harmonica music. This country man had a business to run, and he wanted her help. He wanted to draw her into the madness he'd created by winning the darned Christmas tree contest. "Sam you've been terrific about clearing the driveway, and I hate to turn down your first request for a favor, but I don't think—"

"This doesn't qualify as a favor. The job's too big. I'll pay you. I don't have thousands to spend, but this television special, obnoxious as it may turn out to be, will do wonders for business. Now that I'm in up to my neck, I'd be a fool to skimp on the decorating."

Anna knew that she could use some extra money, especially with all the added expenses of the farmhouse, but still she hesitated. At last she decided to be honest. "I don't know how inspired a job I could do for you, Sam. Lately the thrill has gone out of interior design for me. If I could afford it, I might even quit and hide away in this farmhouse."

"Yeah, I know that feeling. Well, never mind. It was just a thought."

She'd been right to turn him down, she told herself. Quite right. Still, she had trouble dealing with the disappointment in his expression. "Just—um—just what exactly do you need?"

"The television people keep talking about a Norman Rockwell look," he said, brightening at her question.

In spite of herself, Anna began to imagine changes in his parlor. The sofa wasn't bad, although she'd probably recover it, but the armchairs would have to go. The loom, of course, was a perfect detail and should be pulled out, featured somehow. *The loom.*

"Anna, I feel rotten for asking you, but I wouldn't know the first thing about finding another decorator. The job shouldn't take very long, and I'm not picky. I'll also help in any way that—"

"I'll accept the job on one condition," she said, and felt her world expanding, flashing with new color.

"Anything."

"That in exchange I can weave on your grandmother's loom."

2

SAM WAS ENCHANTED with the suggestion. "You've got a deal," he said quickly, watching the transformation in her eyes from guarded reluctance to enthusiastic anticipation. Her agreement to help with the decorating changed his view of the television special. Maybe it wouldn't be so bad, after all.

"I'd like to move the loom over here, if you wouldn't mind," she added.

"Of course." If he'd had some idea that she'd camp in his living room, he'd have to give that up, but it didn't matter. The decorating task would bring them together.

"We'll have to move the loom back in for the filming of the special, though," she said. "A loom with a work in progress would be a terrific addition to the parlor."

"I guess you're right, although what do I know?"

"You don't know a great deal," she teased, "but you're in luck, because I do."

"Evidently." He gestured toward the candlelit table in the dining room. "I feel as if I'm in some fancy restaurant."

"That's because the service is so slow," she said,

laughing. "I'm starving, which means you must be about to faint away from hunger, with all the work you did. Let's eat."

"I'm ready. Need any help?"

"Just carrying a few things in. Right now you can open the wine. The corkscrew's in the far left-hand drawer," Anna said, turning away to open the oven door. Warmth and the aroma of roast chicken filled the kitchen. "Just rummage around."

Finding the corkscrew was easy; he was right at home in this room. He was glad Anna hadn't whirled in here and turned Mrs. McCormick's cozy kitchen into some high-tech wonder. The pine cupboards were still painted antique white. Her blue gingham curtains still hung in the window over the sink, and the refrigerator and enameled stove were the same, too.

He used his pocket knife to peel the covering from the neck of the bottle. "This kitchen sure brings back memories," he said, inserting the curved metal tip of the corkscrew into the cork. "When I was a kid, the lady who lived here used to bake me gingerbread men."

"You grew up here, in Sumersbury?" Anna said, glancing at him.

"No." He thought how wonderful she looked with her cheeks flushed from the heat of the stove. "Just came to my grandparents' house for vacations."

"Then the house you're living in belonged to your grandparents?"

"For nearly fifty years."

"Wow. I'm glad you told me. If anything in that house holds sacred memories for you, I'd better know about it before I start the redesigning project."

"I don't know about 'sacred,' but I'm pretty attached to the stuff there, I guess." He glanced at her, wondering how much to trust her. Finally he said cautiously, "I had a helter-skelter childhood, and the farm and my grandparents were a sort of unchanging center. They became very important to me."

Anna stopped spooning the sauce over the chicken and gave him her full attention, as if she expected him to elaborate. Had she continued working, he wouldn't have, but her respectful pause told him she sincerely wanted to know more about him.

"My parents divorced when I was five," he said, "and Mom remarried...three times. We moved around."

She nodded, seeming to understand without more explanation. "And your father?" she asked gently.

"He disappeared from the scene. I used to hate him for it, but not anymore. My grandmother said he wasn't strong enough to be a part-time father. He wanted all or nothing, so he took nothing. She forgave him for it, and so gradually I did, too."

Anna was silent for a moment. "We'll have to go through that house item by item," she said finally. "You may not even realize the impact of changing something so packed with emotion, but believe me, everyone's surroundings are filled with significance. And yours especially so."

He smiled, feeling a little self-conscious. "Hey, let's not get maudlin. There's plenty of just plain junk over there, too. Besides, I'm not a frightened little boy anymore."

She smiled, too. "Except when it comes to little old ladies from the craft guild."

Sam laughed at the truth of her statement. "You're right. They scared the hell out of me, and I suppose it was because they might trample right over my grandmother and grandfather's stuff." He gazed at Anna. "You must be very good at what you do, even if you are tired of doing it."

She shrugged off his praise. "I've been criticized a few times by the store manager because I supported a client's decision to keep what he already owned instead of buying new furniture. That doesn't move inventory."

"No, but it demonstrates character on your part. Is that why you're ready to give up on your job, because your boss wants you to sell more furniture?"

"No, at least I don't think so. I can handle that." She gazed at him. "I'm not excited about decorating anymore. A client tells me what a wonderful job I've done, and I don't believe him."

"Maybe you need some new directions in your life."

"Maybe I do." The color in her cheeks heightened.

He glanced at the bottle in his hand. "And if I'd ever finish my job, we could drink a toast to that."

"And eat the meal I've promised you," she added, smiling.

"I say we get on with it." Sam pulled the cork from the bottle, and the soft pop it made seemed to herald the beginning of something special. Looking at Anna, her hair creating a celebration of its own as it cascaded down her back and curled around her flushed face, Sam figured that something special had already begun.

During the meal, Anna described her family, all of whom lived in Indiana. Her older brother had a wife and three children, and her mother and father would soon celebrate their thirty-fifth anniversary.

"That's great," Sam commented, sipping his wine. "My grandparents were married sixty-one years, and I sure admire that."

"Did they marry young?" Anna pushed her plate aside and rested her arms on the makeshift tablecloth. "Most couples who make it to a sixtieth anniversary were married young."

"I think they were about twenty. Grandma a little younger, maybe. Yeah," he agreed, chuckling, "some of us will have trouble living long enough to equal that record. Even if I got married tomorrow, I'd have to live to a ripe old ninety-two in order to celebrate a sixtieth anniversary."

"I probably won't make a sixtieth anniversary, either. I'd have to make it to eighty-nine." Anna remembered that she'd once counted her five years with Eric as married years, even though nothing legal had taken place, because Eric had said that he considered himself as married as he'd ever be. "I'll have to leave the long-relationship prizes for my folks and my brother," she added.

"So you're the rebel, huh?" Sam said, teasing her a little.

"If you make some crack about my red hair, I'll be very disappointed in you, Sam."

"Wouldn't dream of it." He sipped his wine and gazed at her over the rim of his glass. "I don't like stereotypes, and besides, my grandmother had red hair, and she was a gentle, loving woman."

"I think you just saved yourself. Maybe I'll unfreeze the Sara Lee cake for dessert, after all."

Sam groaned. "Later, later. I stuffed myself with your delicious supper."

Anna pushed back her chair and picked up their plates. "You'd better not be too stuffed to play your harmonica."

"I was hoping you'd forget."

"Not on your life. Come on," she said, stacking the plates and reaching for her half-full wineglass. "Let's put on jackets and sit on the back porch for a while. You'll feel more at home there, I'll bet, and it will be dark so you won't be self-conscious."

"I don't know why I let you talk me into bringing the thing in the first place," Sam complained, rising from the table.

"Because you're a good neighbor." She grinned over her shoulder as she headed toward the kitchen.

"That must be it." Sam blew out the stubby candles, picked up his own wineglass and followed her. He marveled at her effect on him. In the space of a few hours, she'd coaxed him to reveal the details of his unhappy childhood and persuaded him to play the harmonica for her when he'd never played for a soul but himself.

As Anna put on her nylon jacket and opened the kitchen door leading to the screened porch, she wondered if she'd been too pushy to insist upon her concert. Yet she knew that Sam played well. Oddly enough, he didn't seem to know it. Anna thought it was high time that he did.

The cushions on the metal chairs were cool, the air cooler still. Only a few crickets chirped tonight, and Anna knew that by next weekend they might be gone for the winter. The air smelled like fall—burning leaves and ripe apples. Recently the trees had begun to change color. She looked forward to that each year, always feeling more in tune with autumn than any other season.

Sam chose a chair a distance away from hers, but she understood his shyness.

"It is pretty dark out here," he said, setting his wineglass on a small table. "I won't be able to tell from your expression if you like what I'm playing or not, so you have to stop me the minute you get bored." He pulled the harmonica from his breast pocket.

"I promise."

He blew air through it a few times and tapped it against his hands. Anna suspected that he was stalling, and she continued to wait patiently, wanting the concert as much for him now as for her. At last he began, and her heart constricted with the beauty of the clear notes he played. She recognized the theme from *A Summer Place*, a song he'd played on other evenings.

Sweet, so sweet, she thought, relaxing in the chair as the song wrapped around her. Sam had a gift, and he didn't even recognize it. His playing spoke to her of loneliness and yearning, of tenderness and love. She realized that she knew nothing of his romantic past, but then she'd told him nothing about hers, either. Some things, though, he didn't have to tell her.

He finished the song, and she luxuriated in the feeling it left behind. Then he cleared his throat and tapped the harmonica against his hand again. "Had enough?"

His words jerked her from her romantic haze. "Enough? Oh, Sam, I could listen to you forever. You have no idea how that music lulls me."

"Thought maybe I'd put you to sleep, you were so quiet."

"No, not to sleep. I just feel…comforted, somehow. Please, go on. I know, play 'Unchained Melody.'

That's one of my favorites from listening to you this summer."

"I still can't get over that." His voice, coming to her through the darkness, sounded cozy and intimate. "Me over there, thinking I was all alone while I played, and you over here listening every weekend."

"I guess that's why I feel as if I know you."

He didn't answer, but she sensed a new current of emotion running between them. He was pleased that she liked his playing, she could tell, but his reaction included more than that. She wondered if he understood what was beginning to happen in the seclusion of her darkened porch.

His next song gave her the answer. He knew. Her spine tingled as he played with an awareness that laced the haunting notes of her request.

Anna closed her eyes and pictured Sam as he'd been this afternoon, guiding the heavy chain saw through the fallen tree, heaving the logs into the back of his truck. And now those same hands cradled a silver harmonica against his lips and created magic. She thought of his mouth, supple as it coaxed bell-like tones from the instrument, and she ran her tongue over her lips. She'd expected to enjoy his playing; she hadn't expected it to seduce her.

When he finished, the silence lengthened between them. Anna didn't trust herself to speak, afraid that perhaps she'd indulged in a one-sided fantasy.

He stood up, his form only a dark shadow on the other side of the porch. "It's getting late," he said, his voice sounding thicker than before. "Maybe I'd better head for home."

She pushed herself from her chair and prayed that her legs would support her as she walked toward him. "No cake?"

"Thanks, anyway. I..." He left the unfinished sentence dangling as he stood there, unmoving. Even in the darkness, she knew that he was looking directly at her. "The light from the window is on your hair," he said, almost as if it were an accusation, as if she'd picked that spot to stand on purpose because she knew the light would fall on her hair.

"Oh." Anna stepped out of the light, crazy though it was to do it. She hadn't meant to encourage this untamed feeling between them, and her response to him unsettled her. She suspected that he was grappling with his emotions, too. "Sam," she began unsteadily, "I just..." She couldn't think what to say to him.

"Anna, I—"

She wasn't certain who moved first; perhaps they'd decided at the same instant that the space between them could no longer be tolerated.

"Oh..." She sighed, gazing into his shadowed eyes as his arms drew her to his chest and she felt his heart beat against her breast.

"That about covers it," he murmured, just before he kissed her.

Anna responded with a hunger she hadn't known was there. Sensing it, he deepened the kiss to explore the moist secrets of her mouth. Desire began to churn within her and gain momentum with the sensuous rhythm of his tongue. Helpless before the onset of unexpected passion, she answered him with a moan of delight.

His breathing grew ragged and his body tensed. He rubbed the small of her back and slid his hands over the soft sweat suit material covering her bottom. Slowly he pressed her forward, and when they were tightly locked together, he raised his head to gaze down at her.

"I should have gone home," he murmured.

Anna swallowed. "This isn't what I intended, Sam. But there's something about your music...after listening to it all summer, and then..."

"I don't have that kind of excuse," he said softly, holding her close. "I didn't know that you existed until today."

She held his face with both hands. "Sam," she began, and closed her eyes as another wave of passion made her long to stop talking and kiss him again. She opened her eyes and tried again, determined to overcome her instinctual response to him. "I don't know what's happening, but it could be a number of things. You're a fantasy figure to me, I suppose, after a summer of hearing you play."

"Is there anything wrong with that?" His body throbbed against hers as he reached up and stroked the length of her hair. "Unless you're disappointed with the reality."

"The reality overwhelms me," she said, exploring

the smoothness of his freshly shaved jaw. "But the emotions came so quickly that I don't quite trust them."

"Would you—" he cleared his throat "—would you like me to go?"

She hesitated, torn between reason and desire. "I think so. You see, I don't want this to be the result of loneliness."

"Neither do I. Are you lonely?"

"I didn't think I was. I preferred labels like 'self-sufficient' and 'meditative.' After all, I came to the country specifically to be alone."

Sam was quiet for a moment and finally stepped back, ending the embrace, but his tone remained gentle. "Who is he?"

She stared at him. "What?"

"The guy you came here to forget. Who is he?"

She thought about denying it. After all, no one could prove that buying the house was connected to her breakup with Eric. But she'd just kissed this man with abandon, and perhaps he had a right to know. "I lived with Eric Oretsky for five years, until this past March," she said. "Have you heard of him?"

"No." He sounded morose.

"He's well-known on the New York art scene. We met when I commissioned a painting for the home of a client. I was awed by his fame, and he was—"

"Awed by your beauty," Sam finished. "I can understand. When you walked around the corner of my barn this afternoon, with your hair undone and shining in the setting sun, I was pretty awed myself. Then tonight I discovered that you're sensitive and capable as well as beautiful. Maybe your attraction to me comes from loneliness, but not mine to you. I canceled a date to be here tonight."

"Sam, I had no idea." She felt a pang of guilt.

He shrugged. "No matter. Just wanted you to know that I'm not a lonely country boy, despite those evening harmonica concerts. Was that part of your fantasy?"

"Maybe," Anna admitted, chagrined.

"I play the harmonica for a little while most nights after the chores are done. That doesn't mean that later I don't go out to dinner or maybe even drive to Hartford for a show. As a matter of fact," he added, "sometimes I wish that I could be a little lonelier. Not that my social life is so full, but sometimes I have to meet with clients in the evenings, since I don't have much time during the day."

"'Clients'?" Anna decided that her estimation of Sam had been way off.

"I'm a certified public accountant," he said. "Or that used to be my job description. I was tired of accounting, maybe the same way you're tired of decorating. When I had the chance to run the tree farm, I closed my Hartford office and moved out here, but I still do income tax returns for several people."

"My goodness. And I thought you were totally immersed in the pastoral life."

"I'd love to be, but I can't afford it yet. Maybe, with

the publicity from the White House tree deal, I'll be able to reduce the tax work. That's my goal."

Anna clasped her hands in front of her. "Well," she said, striving for a businesslike tone, "I'd like to help you achieve it, then, by getting the house ready for the cameras."

"Good." He put his hands in the back pockets of his jeans and gazed at her in the dim light. Finally he took a deep breath. "If you ever decide that what you felt a moment ago is something other than loneliness, let me know."

Desire quickened in her again, and she tamped it down. She might very well be reacting to Sam this way because she missed having a man's arms around her, and she didn't want to lead Sam on under those circumstances. "Thank you—for moving the tree... and for understanding."

"Sure thing," he said softly. "When would you like me to bring over the loom?"

"Is tomorrow morning too soon?"

"Not at all."

"And when would you like me to go over the house with you so that I can begin planning what has to be done?" she countered.

He chuckled. "Is tomorrow morning too soon?"

Anna picked up her cue. "Not at all," she said, and they smiled at each other. "I like your style, Sam," she added.

"But maybe you'd feel that way about the first available guy who happened along, is that it?"

Anna sighed. "I'd hate to think so, but... Anyway, you're much more than the 'first available guy.' I already know you're a special person, and it's not as if I don't have opportunities to date in the city. Lord knows my friends have been shoving men at me for months."

Sam considered that. "And by coming out here every weekend, you sidestep their matchmaking efforts, right?"

"Well, I suppose it has that effect."

Sam was quiet for a moment. "I have a suggestion for you," he said at last, "although I may be a damned fool for making it."

"What's that?"

"Why don't you stop running from those city guys and accept a date with the best one of the bunch? See how you react to him."

Anna grimaced. "And if I fall into his arms the way I did yours, I'll know that I'm a lonely old maid desperate for a man—any man."

He chuckled at that. "If you're a lonely old maid, I'm Kermit the Frog."

"Oh, Sam, I don't know," she said, laughing, too. "Keeping clear of men completely was so much easier."

"I think that option's out after tonight," he said gently. "I'll back off, but I don't intend to go away."

She smiled at him. "I'm glad."

"Besides, we have a business arrangement. What time would you like me to deliver the loom?"

"What's your schedule?"

"Light on Saturdays. None of my crew comes to work on weekends except in November and December, when the push is on. I can be here any time after sunup."

"'Sunup.' That has a nice rural ring to it." Taking her cue from Sam, she thrust her hands into her jacket pockets to keep from touching him again. "I still have trouble believing you're a C.P.A."

"Takes all the glamour out of it, I'll bet."

"No, not really." She didn't add that she considered him more intriguing than ever.

"In that case, I'll bring my glamorous self over here, with the loom, about eight o'clock. Is that okay?"

"That's fine. And Sam, am I asking too much to borrow it? Now that I realize how important your grandmother was in your life, I wonder if I have the right to—"

"Anna." He touched her arm with just enough pressure to stop her protestations. Then he withdrew his hand. "In the first place, I can't imagine what harm you could do to the loom, and in the second place, I trust you completely. Your reaction to the loom, your reaction to everything, come to think of it, shows your respect for other people and their possessions."

"That's a nice thing to say."

"Oh, I already have a storehouse of nice things to

say about you, Anna Tilford, but I'm going to save them."

"For a rainy day?" she asked, smiling.

"Maybe. Or a snowy afternoon, or a moonlit night." He turned and headed for the screen door. After opening it, he paused. "Whenever you decide that you're not lonely, after all," he said, and walked down the wooden steps and across the yard to his truck.

Anna opened her mouth to call him back. Did it matter so much why she wanted him tonight? But before she could decide the answer, he'd started the truck's noisy engine, switched on the headlights and driven away.

3

ANNA SET HER ALARM, but she woke before it went off and dressed quickly, shivering with excitement in the early-morning chill. The sun was up, and Sam had promised to arrive soon after. She scampered downstairs and started the coffee. Before it finished perking, she heard Sam's truck in the driveway and hurried to open the front door.

"Mornin'," he called, dropping the tailgate with a metal clang that seemed out of place in the dew-soft air.

Her heart began to pound at seeing him again. She could kid herself that she was excited about finally having a loom, but that wasn't the truth of the matter. She couldn't forget his kiss. "Let me help," she offered, leaving the front door open so they could bring the loom through it.

"I can get it okay. I have a system." He glanced at her and smiled as she approached him. She wondered if he was remembering their kiss, too. "Besides, you'll catch your death out here without a jacket."

"It's not that cold." She looked into his blue eyes and felt certain that he was remembering. Flushing, she glanced up at the loom tied securely in the bed of his pickup. "You polished it, didn't you?"

"Sure. In between answering the phone. It was my dust." He vaulted onto the bed of the truck.

"People called you after you went home last night? It was at least nine-thirty when you left."

"Everyone's so excited, they can't help themselves, I guess." He held out his hand. "Come on, if you're not going back inside. You can steady it from up above while I ease it down the ramp."

She took his warm, outstretched hand but kept her gaze averted as he helped her up beside him. She'd thought that perhaps last night had been the result of the darkness and the music, but this morning they had neither. Her reaction to him was embarrassing, and she tried to cover it by bending to untie the soft ropes holding the loom.

"Okay." Sam slanted two wide boards from the edge of the truck bed to the ground and hopped down. "I wrapped the bottom in pieces of carpeting, so we should be able to slide this baby down the same way I got it up there. You guide from the back, and I'll make sure it doesn't go too fast."

"All right." She helped him work the loom down without incident.

"Now we can carry it between us on into the house. It's not heavy, just bulky. I'll be the one to walk backward. Ready?"

"Ready," Anna said, picking up her end of the

loom. "How on earth did you carry it alone from your house to the truck?"

"I backed the truck as close to the door as I could and laid the boards from the sill to the truck bed," he said, glancing over his shoulder to check their progress.

Anna shook her head. "I didn't have sense enough to realize what I was asking when I blithely suggested you bring the loom over here. I should have been there to help you get it into the truck."

"Nah. It was a challenge."

"Still, I—" She stumbled on a rock, and for one horrible, slow-motion moment, thought she would fall and drop her end of the loom. She didn't.

Sam paused until she regained her balance. "Are you okay?"

"I'm fine," she said, taking a deep breath, "but my life passed before my eyes just now. I'd never forgive myself if something happened to this loom. Maybe my price for being your designer is too high."

"Anna, nothing will happen to this loom, so quit worrying. Now, easy does it up the steps, and we're home free."

Despite his matter-of-fact tone, Anna didn't believe for a minute that her stumbling hadn't scared him. She'd seen the flash of concern and could imagine his heartbreak if the loom had been damaged. Well, it wouldn't be damaged, she vowed as they entered the house.

"Where do you want it?"

"Right here in the parlor is fine." Anna hadn't thought about where she wanted the loom, but she was ready to put it down and end the risk of dropping it. She nodded in the direction of the bay window. "Over by the light."

Sam helped her position the loom so that she would be able to weave and glance out at the wooded area set aside as a nature preserve. Then he surveyed the rest of the room. "You weren't kidding about not decorating this place, were you?"

Anna laughed. "Nope. Looks a little bare, I guess."

"I'll say this, it's uncluttered."

"Considering that the loom is the only piece of furniture so far, I suppose you could call it 'uncluttered.'"

"Shouldn't you at least put up curtains or something?"

"Why?" she teased, saying the first thing that came to her. "I don't run around the house naked."

The moment froze as they stared at each other. She watched Sam's throat move in a convulsive swallow. "Would you...would you like some coffee?" she managed at last.

His tone was strained. "Sure."

"Anything else?" Her face grew hot. "I mean, like breakfast? I have eggs and bacon and some—"

"Coffee will be fine," he said, the tightness still in his voice. "The bench for the loom is still in the truck. I'll get it while you pour the coffee."

They each bolted from the room in different directions. In the kitchen, Anna held her hands to her burning cheeks. Had her comment about running around naked been a Freudian slip? Was she trying so hard to hide her attraction to Sam that her interest popped out in other ways? She must not appear to be flirting with him or leading him on, unless she was prepared to follow through. And following through, before she understood herself better, was a frightening prospect.

Out at the truck, Sam paused to take several long, steadying breaths. Anna had made herself clear last night; she didn't want to start a relationship on the rebound. He didn't want her to do that, either. So he had to control himself around her and keep everything light and friendly.

He'd managed well until she blurted out that insane comment about running around naked and followed it by asking him if he wanted anything besides coffee from her. Hell, yes, he wanted something besides coffee.

But he didn't relish the idea of becoming the guy she used to forget her old boyfriend. Her own doubts about her attraction to him had to be cleared away before anything more happened between them. In the meantime, he hoped she wouldn't make any more statements that sent his imagination into forbidden territory. He opened the passenger side of the cab and took out the bench he'd propped upside down on the seat.

When he brought it into the house, Anna met him

in the bare parlor with two mugs of coffee. To an observer, they might be newlyweds moving into their first house, he thought, and quickly banished the fantasy. He placed the bench in front of the loom and accepted the coffee with a smile of thanks.

"I still can't believe the loom is here, in my house," she said, caressing the polished wood with her free hand. "Look how the light from the window makes the wood glow."

Sam, fool that he was, noticed how the light from the window made her fiery hair glow. "I had it back in a corner, covered with dust," he said. "I'm glad it's not still there."

"Wait until you see it with a weaving in progress. I don't know which I love more, the beauty of a loom or the colors of the yarn." She sipped her coffee and gazed at the empty loom, as if imagining the wonders she would produce on it.

"The way you talk about weaving, I'm surprised you haven't bought your own loom by now."

"I should have. I surely should have." She glanced at him. "Have you ever been around someone with a personality so forceful that you loose track of who you are, what you want from life?"

"No, can't say that I have. Your boyfriend?"

She nodded. "Maybe it happens to women more than men. When Eric came into my life, he took over everything, it seems to me now. His work crowded into every corner of my apartment. There was no room for anything else, and he was so good—a genius some said—that I didn't feel I had the right to protest."

"So now you live in a nearly empty house in the country. There's space all around you."

She gazed at him. "Space for a loom. Finally."

"Sounds like it's about time," he said, wondering silently if there was space for him, as well. "I guess this was all a happy accident."

"I think it was, Sam. And we mustn't forget the rest of the bargain. When you've finished your coffee, I'm ready to tour your house and begin planning the re-designing project."

"Wouldn't you rather buy some yarn and get started on the loom? Tessie Johanson has a yarn shop in town, and she's open Saturdays, I think."

"I've noticed that shop, and I'll go there this after-noon, but a deal is a deal, Sam. The sooner we go over what needs to be done with your house, the more time ideas will have to ferment in my brain. I can think while I weave, once I know what we're up against."

Sam drained his cup. "Then let's go. We'll take my truck."

"If you don't mind, I'll follow in my car. Then I can go on from there into town."

"I'd be glad to take you into—" he began, and caught himself. Not twenty minutes ago he'd vowed to go slow with Anna. Now he was on the verge of taking her shopping for yarn, and next he'd suggest threading the loom together, sharing supper again, sharing... He had to get hold of himself. "I guess you're right," he said. "It would be simpler if you followed me in your car. Ready to go?"

"I'll get my jacket."

As Anna followed Sam's truck down the country road bordering their properties, she reminded herself that Sam was a client, the same as her customers in New York, and she owed him her professional best. A great deal was on the line for him; not many of her clients faced national television coverage of their redecorated home.

She didn't feel like a professional this morning, perhaps because she was traveling to this consultation dressed in lavender sweats rather than a beige business suit. Instead of the slim briefcase that usually rested on the seat beside her, she had a legal pad and ballpoint pen. To make matters even more informal, she'd bartered her services for the use of a floor loom. Good old-fashioned Yankee horse trading, she thought with a smile.

Nevertheless, she couldn't treat this job any differently from all the others she'd taken on through the years. She'd give Sam his money's worth, or his loom's worth, in this case. After parking her car, she walked over to where he waited by his truck.

"How much of the house will we be concerned with?" she asked as they crossed the small covered porch and he opened the unlocked front door.

"I think all of it, unfortunately. Bedrooms, kitchen, parlor, dining room, maybe even the bathroom, for all I know. I could close a door or two, I suppose, but that would look—"

"Tacky," Anna finished for him. "I agree. If cameras will be snooping everywhere, let's make sure we cover every detail. If you don't mind, let's start upstairs with the bedrooms and work down."

"Fine with me." He led the way through the parlor and started up the creaking wooden stairs to the second floor. The stairway had been built in two sections, with a small landing in between. "There are three bedrooms and one bathroom," he explained, pausing on the landing and turning to make room for her there. "About like your upstairs, I guess."

"It's similar," she agreed, "except that my stairs aren't constructed this way. They just go straight up."

"Ah, too bad. This was my favorite spot as a kid. Let me show you something." He squatted next to a door about two feet square set into the narrow wall beside the landing.

"What is it?" Anna leaned down as he opened the small door.

"My cubbyhole." Sam reached inside and pulled out a dusty rectangular box. "Here's Parcheesi," he said, setting the box on the floor in front of him, "and here's Kentucky Derby," he added, placing another box with taped corners on top of the first. "I loved that one. You roll the dice and move the horses along the track." He lifted the lid and one corner split through the tape.

"Did your grandparents build this into the wall for you, or was it always here?"

"I think it's always been here, but not necessarily for toys. I can still remember the day my grandmother took me by the hand and showed me this little door. The old toys were already in there, but from time to time she'd add a new one, like this, for instance." He held up a detailed model of a hook and ladder truck. "She bought that when I announced that I wanted to be a fireman."

"Your grandmother was really something, wasn't she?"

"Quite simply, she taught me what love was," he said, gazing at her.

"I can see that."

He held her gaze for a moment longer and then broke the contact. "I suppose we'd better put these back. We have things to do," he said, replacing the items. "Unless I can interest you in a game of Kentucky Derby?" he asked with a chuckle.

"I'd like that sometime," she said. "How long since you've played?"

"At least twenty years," he said, closing the door and rising to his feet. "But that doesn't matter. There's no skill involved. Winning depends on the roll of the dice. It's pretty simplistic."

"That could be a relief," Anna replied, remembering how with Eric, games had to be tests of intellect. When she lost, she felt diminished. When he lost, he sulked.

"Then it's a date," Sam said. "One evening soon we'll take Kentucky Derby down by the fire, pop popcorn and act like kids."

She opened her mouth to agree and then changed her mind. Hadn't she just lectured herself about not jumping into things with Sam? "We'll see," she said.

He met her statement with a moment of silence. "All right," he said finally. "We'll see." Then he held out his hand toward the next set of steps. "Ready to go on?"

She'd hurt his feelings, right after he'd given her a revealing glimpse of his lonely childhood. She cringed. "I'm sorry if I can't—"

"Anna, it's okay," he interrupted. "You handle things the way you have to. Now let's get on with the tour."

Wanting to overcome her misgiving yet unable to, she followed him up the stairs.

"My grandfather told me these two houses were built around 1820 by a couple of brothers," he said over his shoulder. "And supposedly twenty years after that the brothers sold out, packed up their families and headed west."

"I wondered if the real estate agent was making that up, but the houses look to be about the same age." She was glad he didn't sound upset about her semirejection.

"Well, I hope the story's true, because the TV people wanted to know how old my house was, and when I said almost 170 years, they went nuts."

"I'll bet."

"I explained that I lived alone and hadn't paid much attention to how the place looked." He stopped in the hallway and waited for her to join him.

"And what did they say to that?"

"They patiently suggested that because I had a chance for free national coverage that would put my Christmas tree farm on the map, that maybe I'd be smart to pay some attention to how the place looked." He grinned at her. "I saw their point."

"Smart fellow." Anna flipped her hair back from her shoulder and uncapped her pen. "Then I guess we'll start with this hall. It's pretty dark and dingy, and the wallpaper..." She paused, remembering that she had to be careful. "Did your grandmother choose this wallpaper?"

"Yep."

"How much do you love it?"

Sam laughed and stuck his hands in his back pockets. "I don't. She got the stuff on sale, and my grandfather and I put it up one summer, telling her the whole time that maroon wallpaper with pink peonies would look awful in this hall. Once we'd finished, she hated it, too, but none of us were in the mood to peel it off again."

"I can understand that. Wallpaper is no fun to take off."

"Especially if you don't care that much. As my grandparents grew older, they minded less and less that the wallpaper was ugly or the furniture didn't match. They both were great readers, and their focus shifted away from their surroundings, except for my grandmother and her loom. That was sort of a spiritual thing for her, too, in a way. She claimed that weaving helped her think."

Anna remembered the peaceful times she'd spent in front of a loom and had to agree. "You don't care much about your surroundings, either, do you?" she asked.

"Will I be in trouble if I say I don't? After all, we're talking about your profession."

Anna shrugged. "If I had a choice between someone who's unconcerned about their surroundings and someone who demands that the washcloths and towels all match, I'll take the first type." She smiled at him. "Besides, just because you don't feel like tackling the job yourself, doesn't mean you won't enjoy the finished product."

Sam leaned against the wall and gazed at her. "It won't be the same house, though, will it?"

"Not really," she answered honestly. "We're dealing with change in a very personal part of your life, the rooms where you live."

"I'm beginning to understand that. After you're finished, I'll be living with the results of your work. Your influence, your presence, will be all around me."

"Well, I—" She felt the heat in her cheeks once more. "No one's ever put it quite that way before. Most of my clients like to think the final effect will reflect their tastes, not mine. I just bring their tastes into focus."

"But I don't have any particular tastes."

"Yes, you do. You only think you don't. The wallpaper, for example. We'll have to strip it. What would you like in its place?"

"Beats me."

"Come on, now, Sam. Use your imagination."

"Well, a light color, maybe. Cream or white, to make the space bigger."

"Exactly. That wasn't so hard, was it?"

"Nope. I'll strip the wallpaper and repaint the hall myself, if that helps."

"It'll help your budget, for one thing." Anna scribbled a few notes on her legal pad. "Then let's move on to the bedrooms, master bedroom first."

"Okay. At the end of the hall." He gestured for her to precede him to a half-open door that faced the stairs.

"Is it your room?"

"Now. Used to be my grandparents'."

"And there are things in here that are more important to you than maroon wallpaper," she guessed, stepping inside the light-filled room.

"That's right."

"A sleigh bed," Anna murmured, walking over to run her hand along the footboard railing. The bed and matching double dresser, which she suspected were walnut, had been covered with a layer of deep blue paint. An ivory spread that had seen better days was tucked in around the double mattress and box spring nestled into the curving side rails.

"The bed stays," Sam announced from behind her.

"Oh, absolutely. Sleigh beds are wonderful. I've always loved them."

"And never owned one?"

"No." She turned toward him with a self-deprecating smile. "Once again, by the time I could afford it, I was involved with someone who insisted we have a futon."

"There's quite a difference between a futon and a sleigh bed." He leaned in the doorway, watching her.

"I know. Futons are comfortable and practical, but I longed for something more...encompassing, more solid." She hadn't meant to say that. She hadn't meant to get into this conversation at all. The discussion about toys had softened her up, and now they were trading ideas about beds.

He glanced at her, his blue eyes warm with thoughts that probably echoed hers.

"Dammit, Sam, I'm attracted to you, okay?"

He grinned. "And you're furious at me because of it."

"That's silly. Of course I'm not!"

"Of course you're not," he said mildly.

"I'm having trouble, that's all, trying to keep my head when you're so charming, and you show me your childhood toys, and we discuss the merits of sleigh beds."

"Then I take it you don't want to hear about the

hours of fun I had as a kid playing pirates in this bed?"

"No."

"Or pioneer, and the bed was my covered wagon?"

"Stop it, Sam. I don't want to like you so much, so fast."

His smile was infectious. "Too bad for you."

"Probably."

Had he moved toward her then and taken her in his arms, she wouldn't have been able to stop whatever would happen. Seduced by his teasing, she'd lost track of her resolve to keep her distance. Had he pulled her down to the sleigh bed and whispered words of desire, she would have stayed with him there. But he remained leaning in the doorway. Gradually the moment passed.

"Who painted the furniture blue?" she asked finally.

"My grandmother. When we check out the other bedrooms, you'll see that she went through a 'blue phase.' Why?"

"I...think the bed would look better refinished in its natural color."

"We can do that. No problem. Tom Carey down at the hardware store refinishes antiques on the side. He's always told me to holler if I wanted any of my grandparents' stuff restored. I don't think he'll charge too much, either."

"Good. Then we may as well have him do the dresser, too. I'm not going to suggest refinishing everything, because it would be very expensive, but these two pieces will make a strong statement." She glanced at him. "You may have to sleep with the mattress on the floor for a while."

"I can bed down anywhere. That's one thing I learned in all my moving around as a kid."

"Then that's settled." Anna decided they'd had entirely enough talk about beds and bedding down. Crossing the room, she examined the armchair and ottoman. The slipcovers, a blue-and-green print that had faded where the sun streamed through the window onto the fabric, would have to be replaced, as would the bedspread. One item in the room, however, was perfect the way it was. Across the chair, tossed there nonchalantly, was a stunning woven blanket in shades of blue.

Anna laid her pen and legal pad on the chair and fingered the soft tweed pattern. As a designer and a former weaver, she marveled at the intricate use of colors. "Your grandmother made this blanket, didn't she?" Anna knew the answer.

"Yes." He left the doorway and came to stand beside her. "As a gift to my grandfather, to wrap up in on cold winter evenings while he was reading in front of the fire. My—my grandmother died before he did, and this blanket kept her near."

"For you, too."

"For me, too."

"The work is exquisite." She glanced up at him. "Your grandmother had a real gift for weaving."

"I think you might have the same gift."

"I have no idea. I didn't stay with it long enough to find out. But if I could produce something as fine as this, I'd be very proud."

"It's probably the best thing she ever did, but as we go through the house, I'll show you some others. I dry dishes with the tea towels she wove," he added.

"You *do*? How could you bear to?"

"Because that's what she made them for. They'll last for years if they're handwoven. She never wanted to spend her time on wall hangings. Instead she wove stuff people could use every day, things people would touch and feel the texture of the material."

"A sensuous woman," Anna murmured before realizing that might not be the comment a grandson would want to hear. "What I mean is—"

"I know what you mean," he said. "And you're right. She was alive to all that life had to offer."

Anna understood his implication. "That's a wonderful trait," she said, speaking more from nervousness than need. "She must have been..." His light touch on her hair stopped the flow of words. She gazed at him while he combed gently through the loose curls. "You shouldn't be doing that, Sam."

"I know."

In a moment he would kiss her. The emotions generated by the presence of the sleigh bed hadn't disappeared, they'd only gone underground temporarily. Her heartbeat was loud in her ears, louder than the chirp of birds in the tree outside the window.

The sunlight streaming into the room flecked Sam's blue eyes with gold as he gazed down at her. "I know you want to take this slow. I keep trying to remember, but when you're right here, so close..."

She was lost and she knew it. He would kiss her and she would kiss him back. The attraction was too strong, the reasons for waiting too flimsy. Slowly he leaned toward her.

4

THE KNOCKING at the front door didn't penetrate to either of them at first, but before Sam's mouth touched hers, he heard it and straightened. "The door," he said dully. "Someone's at the door."

"You'd better answer it."

The knocking continued, and a woman called out for Sam. "Yoo-hoo, Sammy! It's Estelle Terwiliger, dear."

Sam closed his eyes. "I should have known when she didn't call this morning that she'd show up at my door, instead."

"Go and talk with her." Anna picked up her pen and legal pad. "I'll work up here while you—"

"No," he said, cupping her elbow and steering her toward the bedroom door. "We may as well let her know you're redecorating the house. This is as good a time as any. By the way, does she know you're an interior designer?"

"No, at least not as of yesterday. Word spreads so fast around here, she may know my life story by now."

"Not from me." Sam ushered her down the stairs.

"Won't she be disappointed that she's not in charge?"

He sighed. "Yeah, she will. I'll have to come up with some way to mollify her, but I want her to see that I've hired a professional for the job."

Some professional, Anna thought, and straightened the front of her sweat suit as she reached the bottom of the stairs. Would Estelle Terwiliger wonder why Sam had taken so long to answer her knock? Anna smoothed her hair and gave thanks that Estelle hadn't arrived a few minutes later.

Sam opened the door, and Estelle blocked most of the light coming through it. "Why there you are, Sammy! I was driving by and thought I'd stop in and chat about your house and the TV special. The guild is so excited about this."

"Come in, Estelle." He stepped back from the door. "I'm glad you're here. I guess you've met Anna."

Estelle nodded in Anna's direction. "Just yesterday, at the grocery."

"You'll never believe what she does for a living, Estelle," Sam continued. "She's an interior designer."

"Why, how nice." Estelle clutched the handle of her appliquéd purse against her stomach while she studied Anna with guarded interest. "I didn't think you knew Sammy."

"I—" Anna began, not sure how to explain.

"She came by yesterday to see if I could help with that red maple that was blocking her driveway," Sam interjected smoothly. "When I found out she was an interior designer, I immediately thought that's what we needed, a professional to take care of the inside of the house so that the rest of us can concentrate on the other details. Don't you think so, Estelle?"

"Well, I don't know, Sammy. Naturally, I thought that the guild would redo your house for you." She glanced around the parlor. "Gertie has a lovely oil painting she did a few years ago that would go nice over the fireplace, and Gertie said she'd even sell it, if someone saw it on TV and wanted to have a genuine piece of folk art. And of course, Edwina makes those wooden geese in funny poses, and..."

"All that would have been fine," Sam commented when Estelle paused for a breath. "But I don't see how you ladies would have time, considering all that has to be done in connection with the tree-cutting ceremony. So Anna will handle this little job, and you can concentrate on the other plans."

Estelle stared at him with her mouth slightly open, and Anna marveled at his diplomacy. She wondered if he had any idea what other "plans" he was talking about.

"Uh, I guess so, Sammy," Estelle said. "You'll have to refresh my memory about what else we've planned. My mind's been so occupied with fixing up this house that I forgot about the rest."

"Well, there's the—the town choir, for one thing."

"What town choir? We don't have a town choir, just the Congregational choir and the Methodist choir, and of course the high school choir, but no town choir."

"There, you see? Who's going to organize all those groups into one unit for the carols? And I would say, when the cameras go out into the woods to film the tree cutting, we ought to have carols by the Sumersbury Town Choir."

Anna gazed at Sam in wonder and hoped that he knew what he was doing. What if the network didn't want carolers tramping around, drowning out the commentary?

Estelle nodded, a gleam in her eye. "I can see it now, carolers in hats and scarves, carrying candles—"

"This will be in daylight, Estelle," Sam reminded her, "but you're getting the idea."

"And an organ! Ernest has that small one in his parlor. We could load it onto the back of a truck, maybe your truck, Sammy, and get a long extension cord... Yes, I can imagine the organ music through the pines...."

Sam's brow creased and he glanced at Anna, who brought the legal pad up to hide her smile of amusement. Sam had jumped into some rough water, she thought.

"Maybe not an organ, Estelle," he said hesitantly. "An extension cord hasn't been made that would reach all the way up to—"

"Nonsense, Sammy! We have to have an organ. Do

you think the 'Hallelujah Chorus' would be appropriate, right as you begin to cut the tree?"

"Um, I think the noise of the saw might—"

"Quite right. We'll sing the 'Hallelujah' right after the tree crashes down. In fact, the high school trumpet section could join the organist for that."

Sam sent Anna a look of alarm as Estelle rattled on.

"Or maybe a solo would be more effective. The 'Ave Maria,' perhaps. I'm very good at singing the 'Ave Maria.' You've heard me, haven't you, Sammy? Tell Anna how impressive that Christmas Eve service was last year at the Congregational Church."

"It was something, all right," Sam agreed, looking panicked, "but I wonder if—"

"Leave the details to me," Estelle said, turning toward the door. "We'll make Sumersbury the talk of the country!" She whisked out the door. "Nice seeing you again, Anna," she called over her shoulder as she hurried down the front steps.

Sam closed the door quietly behind her and turned to Anna. "My God, what have I done?"

"Exactly what you wanted to do," she said, chuckling. "You've mollified Estelle Terwiliger. Who is she, anyway? She acts as if she's in charge of the world."

"She's in charge of this little corner of it," Sam replied. "Estelle is the senior member of the town council, president of the DAR, founder and president of the Sumersbury Craft Guild and chairwoman of every charity drive in town."

"Wow."

"Nobody in Sumersbury wants to tangle with her. Besides, she's a good old gal, really. The town wouldn't function without her. But good Lord, now she's gonna have the whole blasted population trampling through my Christmas tree farm singing the 'Hallelujah Chorus'! With trumpets!"

"Maybe not." Anna knew she shouldn't laugh at his distress, but she couldn't help it. "Maybe she'll go with the 'Ave Maria' solo, instead."

Sam groaned. "That would be worse. Estelle's singing has been compared to raccoons mating. Ever hear that?"

"Can't say that I have."

"Well, if she sings the 'Ave Maria' at the tree cutting ceremony, you'll think you're in the middle of *Wild Kingdom*, believe me."

"Oh, Sam." She couldn't contain her laughter any longer. "All this so that the Sumersbury Craft Guild won't put wooden geese in your living room."

"Yeah." He began to chuckle. "Well, you haven't seen the geese, either."

Anna laughed harder. "What does she mean, 'in funny poses'?"

"Don't ask." His laughter joined hers. "I don't care," he said, shaking his head. "I really don't care. I'll take the 'Hallelujah Chorus' and the 'Ave Maria' if it means you'll be decorating the house instead of Estelle Terwiliger."

She wiped her eyes. "You know, we haven't made

much progress in that regard. We've only covered the hall and one bedroom."

"Ask me if I care about that, either. The longer it takes, the more I can be with you."

She gazed at him and her smile faded. "Sam, we've got to slow down. When Estelle was here I was shocked to realize that I'd met you yesterday. *Yesterday*."

"Time isn't always the crucial factor."

"Maybe not, but I need more of it."

"Okay," he said softly. "I won't push."

"Let's cover the downstairs now. We can save the other two bedrooms for next weekend. Everything doesn't have to be decided today."

"Look, I can go back upstairs with you without causing any problems, if that's what you're worried about. I can control myself."

"It's not you I'm worried about," she said.

"That gives me hope."

"Please don't pin hopes on me, Sam. Not yet. I think you're right about my needing to date someone in the city and find out how I react."

"I was afraid I'd live to regret that suggestion."

"No, it's a good idea, the sort of advice a friend would give, and I appreciate the thought."

Sam frowned. "Me and my big mouth. I've opened it twice too many times in the past twenty-four hours. I just hope what I said to you doesn't end up the same way as my suggestion to Estelle. I have single-handedly turned that woman into a runaway train."

"Maybe not. The network might love what she's cooking up."

Sam eyed her dubiously. "Yeah, and I'm the Prince of Wales."

"Let's just say you're a prince," she said, and before he could respond, she walked into the parlor and began making notes on her pad. "Now, the sofa can stay, but it needs reupholstering."

"You're the boss," he said.

She had a feeling he wasn't referring to interior design.

THEY WERE INTERRUPTED by several phone calls, and they'd barely completed their survey of the downstairs when a man arrived who seemed to know Sam well. The man asked if Sam would help him cart home a riding lawn mower he'd bought that morning. Anna was amazed that the man would buy the lawn mower and then ask Sam to transport it in his truck. But Sam appeared perfectly happy to do the favor.

Despite his impatience with all the phone calls, he liked this small-town attitude of give-and-take, she realized. His behavior was very different from the private, independent postures adopted by the people she knew in the city. When she'd bought the farmhouse, she'd imagined that it would give her more privacy, but if she became involved with Sam Garrison, she'd probably have far less. The concept made her uncomfortable. Good thing, she thought, that she'd told Sam she needed more time. Time and space.

Sam left with the man who'd bought the lawn mower, and Anna drove into town. After stopping at Sumersbury's only lunch counter for a sandwich and a cup of coffee, she headed for Tessie Johanson's yarn shop. Her fingers itched to begin weaving.

A bell jangled when she opened the door, and a tall, handsome woman in her fifties came out of the back room wiping her mouth with a cloth napkin. She looked like someone who should be named Tessie Johanson, Anna thought, with her Slavic cheekbones and her blond-gray hair swept into a coil on top of her head.

"I've interrupted your lunch," Anna apologized. "I can come back later."

"Heavens no, don't do that." The woman's wide mouth curved into a smile. "I need the customers more than I need the lunch."

"I suppose it might be hard to keep a business going in a town as small as Sumersbury," Anna said, admiring the rainbow of yarns arranged in diamond-shaped bins on the wall. "You are the owner, right?"

"Right. I'm Tessie." She held out her hand.

"I'm Anna Tilford." Anna grasped the woman's hand firmly. "I bought the McCormick place." Anna had found people in Sumersbury related better to a name than an address.

"Oh, so you're the one. Nobody seemed to know."

"I'm the one," Anna said with a smile. "And on top

of that, I've borrowed my neighbor's loom. I'm here to buy yarn and hopefully get some advice."

Tessie's eyebrows shot up. "Sam Garrison is letting you use his grandmother's loom?"

"That's right."

"I'm impressed. I tried to buy that loom from him, and he wouldn't sell. He said it would be like selling off a memory, and I could understand that. A lot of Hilary Schute's personality was tied in with her loom."

Hilary, Anna thought, liking the name. "You knew her?"

"Very well. She was the only serious weaver in town besides me. She's the one who encouraged me to open this shop, and she was my best customer until the cancer got so bad that weaving was impossible."

"From what you and Sam have told me, she must have been quite a lady. I've seen some of her work."

Tessie nodded. "You're lucky to be using her loom. You'll get good vibes from it."

"I believe you."

"Tell me if this is too personal, but how did this come about, that you have use of it? Did you know Sam before you bought the McCormick place?"

Anna considered her answer. She'd been right; there weren't many secrets in a small town.

"Never mind," Tessie said as Anna hesitated. "Bad habit of mine. I dig into the personal history of everyone who buys yarn or takes lessons from me. It doesn't matter why you have the loom. What sort of yarn and advice do you need?"

Anna relaxed and decided to tell her story anyway. Tessie would find out soon enough that her new customer was redecorating Sam's house for the television special. "The loom is part of some Yankee horse trading," she said. "I'm an interior designer, and I'm trading my skills in exchange for use of the loom. Sam's trying to get ready for this special, you know."

"Oh, my, don't I ever. But I thought Estelle Terwiliger and her gang were doing Sam's house."

"They'll be doing...other things, instead," Anna said, trying not to smile.

"Like what?"

"Um, I think they'll organize a town choir, and—"

"A what?"

"For the tree cutting ceremony," Anna said, struggling to keep a straight face. "You know, to sing carols, and maybe the 'Hallelujah Chorus,' or maybe Mrs. Terwiliger will sing a solo."

"Saints preserve us." Tessie looked at her with wide eyes. "Whose idea was that?"

"I—uh—think it was Sam's."

The dazed look slowly cleared from Tessie's face. "That sly dog. He diverted Estelle and her cronies away from his house and hired you. The trouble is, he's turned that woman loose on the entire town."

"Maybe it won't be so—"

"Ah, you don't know Estelle Terwiliger like I do. We'll have a Cecil B. deMille production organized by the first week in December, with all of us appointed to play our respective parts. I figured the house would keep her busy, but now that you're doing that, she's going to run amok." Tessie began to smile. "You know, it'll be hysterical, if I can keep my sense of humor and ignore what the rest of the nation thinks of Sumersbury after this. My, my." She shook her head and chuckled. "But this discussion isn't getting you started on your first project, is it?"

"I guess not, and I'm only here on weekends, so—"

"Heavens! You should have said so immediately. Do you think you remember how to thread a loom?"

"Pretty much."

Tessie fished for a stack of papers under the counter. "Here's a handout I use when I teach weaving, although I've only had a few classes and nobody's stayed with it except Hilary. Most of the women in town, or even surrounding towns, for that matter, would rather knit or crochet. The initial outlay is less, and needles don't take up floor space."

Anna glanced at the step-by-step diagram of threading a loom, and the technique came back to her as if she'd been weaving only yesterday. "Yes, yes, I remember," she said, growing excited. "And the counting and measuring and deciding on a pattern, and tying up the treadles. I had a full semester's course in college."

"Do you have a warping board?"

"No," Anna said, looking up in alarm. "That thing with the pegs that you wind your warp thread on? I didn't even think to ask Sam. I have forgotten some things, after all."

"Never mind. No telling where Hilary's is, so I'll loan you one of mine." She hurried to the back room and reappeared in no time with a square frame dotted with pegs. "Now remember how you wind the yarn on this for the warp, and transfer it to the loom," she said. "Wait a minute. I may have another handout." She rummaged under the counter and came up with a second stack of papers.

"This is great of you, Tessie. I feel as if I ought to pay for lessons, with all the help you're giving me."

"Forget it. I'm delighted someone's using Hilary's loom again."

"You sound like Sam. Is everyone in Sumersbury so neighborly?"

Tessie laughed. "Most of us, I guess. Of course, along with the neighborliness comes nosiness."

"Oh, well," Anna said, laughing with her. "Can't have everything."

"That's what my husband and I decided, so we chose the friendliness of a small town, and we accept that we have no secrets from anybody." She cocked her head and gazed at Anna. "Maybe if you're only here on weekends, you'll be able to keep a few of your secrets."

"I doubt it," Anna said with a smile.

"Anyway, getting back to your warping and threading of the loom, you'll probably be fine, but if you'd like me to come out and get you started, say so.

I'd consider it an honor to help someone set up on Hilary's loom."

"Thanks, but I'd like to try it myself first. If I land in real trouble, I'll let you know."

"Anytime. My home phone's on both sheets, as well as the shop number. I don't go out much. I stay home and weave."

"Sounds nice." Anna glanced around the shop and wondered if weaving and owning a yarn shop like this one would be an alternative to interior design. Of course, she wouldn't be able to have a shop in Sumersbury. From Tessie's opening comment about needing the business more than lunch, and the absence of other customers, Anna concluded that even one yarn shop in Sumersbury might be one too many.

"What's the first thing you plan to make?" Tessie asked.

Anna had thought about that. "A tablecloth and napkins," she said, remembering her panic when she'd tried to set a pretty table for Sam the night before.

"I'd start on the napkins. They'll be easier."

"Good advice." Anna soaked up the warm encouragement and camaraderie. Tessie had the right idea about becoming involved with her customers. Anna realized that she did the same thing in her work, or at least she had in the beginning. Lately she'd lost her enthusiasm for doing so. Maybe she was burned-out, after all.

Before long she left the shop carrying a paper bag

stuffed with lavender, light blue and turquoise yarn and another handout that detailed the threading for various types of weaving patterns. The next time Sam ate at her house, he would use handwoven table linens.

She caught herself up short. Was she already planning another meal involving Sam? She argued with herself that she was using his loom and that logically she should want to show off her first project to the owner of the loom. But that wasn't it. She knew full well it wasn't.

As she drove past Sam's place, she glanced through the rows of baby Christmas trees and noticed that his truck was parked in front of his house. He must have finished helping his friend haul the mower home. She thought about stopping to tell him about her conversation with Tessie Johanson and her success with buying yarn and getting enough information to begin her first project. She decided against it. Better to leave well enough alone for now.

When she stepped out of the car in her newly cleared driveway, she heard the sound of someone chopping wood behind her house. Her heartbeat sped up. Only one person would be chopping her firewood, yet why was his truck still at home? She carried her bag of yarn and Tessie's warp board around to the back of the house.

Sure enough, he was there, reminding her of a lumberjack as he swung the sledgehammer in an arc over his head and drove the wedge through a section of thick trunk. The wood split with a sharp crack, and the two halves thudded to either side of the chopping block.

As he reached for one of them to split it in half again, he saw her. "Hi. Thought I'd get this out of the way for you, in case you want a fire soon."

"That's very nice of you, but how did you get here? I saw your truck parked in front of your house." She flushed slightly when she realized that he'd know she'd taken the time to check.

"The back path." He pointed toward a spot in the nearby woods that she hadn't noticed before, a spot a few feet to the right of an outcropping of granite. "It's much shorter than going by the road, although it's grown over a lot since Mrs. Mac died, and nobody's used it to get between the two houses."

Her pulse quickened at the thought of a backwoods path between their houses. The path linked them with a shared secret. "How long has it been there?"

"Forever, I guess." He leaned on the sledgehammer. "The brothers who built these two houses probably cleared it as a shortcut for all the times they went back and forth and the wives visited and the cousins played together."

She smiled. "It's fun to think of all the people who walked through these woods, and why."

"Yeah, it is. When Mrs. Mac died, I wondered if that was the end of using the path. I mean, without your permission, I'd be trespassing to walk over here through your property."

She smiled. "Well, you certainly have permission to walk along that path, Sam."

"So do you." He gazed at her steadily.

"Uh, thanks," she murmured, feeling warm. "It will come in handy, I imagine, while we're working on your house."

"I imagine." He continued to lean on the sledge-hammer and gaze at her.

She swallowed and looked away. He had a powerful pull in those blue eyes. "You know, Sam, I feel guilty having you split this wood today. You already spent time helping that man with his mower, and I'm sure that you—"

"Wanted an excuse to come over and find out how you made out at the yarn shop with Tessie," he finished.

She was disconcerted by his honesty. "I made out fine," she said.

"Looks like you came home with a bag full of yarn and a warp board. I forgot about that part, and I don't know where my grandmother's is."

"That's okay. Tessie loaned me this one," she said, relaxing a little now that they were discussing weaving and not a secret path between their houses. "Tessie was a wonderful help, and she had some nice things to say about your grandmother, too."

"Yeah, they were good buddies. Was she surprised that you've got the loom?"

"Yes, a little."

"Did you tell her about our deal?"

"Yes, I did. I hope you don't mind, but some explanation seemed necessary."

He laughed. "Some explanation usually is in Sumersbury. You've managed to keep clear of the local residents all summer, but they've been dying to know about the new owner of the McCormick place. I'm afraid your privacy is jeopardized now that you've made contact."

"The television special would have done that eventually, anyway," she said without rancor. Her private country retreat would never be the same, but maybe that was okay. Maybe she was ready to gradually enter the community of Sumersbury. Knowing Tessie Johanson would be a definite plus. And then there was Sam...and the secret path that linked his property with hers.

"Probably. I'm sorry, Anna. Things got out of hand."

"I'm not sorry. Not anymore."

He absorbed her statement and smiled. "Good." Then he picked up the sledgehammer. "Now, if you're anything like my grandmother, you're impatient to thread that loom with your new yarn. Don't let me keep you from doing that. What're you making first?"

"A tablecloth and napkins. I can't be using sheets and paper napkins forever."

He arched one eyebrow. "Sounds like you might be settling into this house a little."

"I—maybe."

"That's good, too."

She stood there, undecided about what to do. He was working so hard for her. Should she invite him for another meal? Yet if she did after what had already happened between them, she'd be indicating a willingness for more than she was ready for. "Sam, you've done so much for me, and I should probably—"

"Hey, stop right there. 'Should' has no part in whatever happens between us." He smiled gently. "I have a date tonight, Anna. Does that help?"

5

SAM HAD A DATE, Anna thought sadly as brightness drained from her day. "Yes, that helps," she said. "Thank you for splitting the wood, Sam."

"You're welcome. Now get in there and bring that loom alive. I know you can."

"All right." She turned and walked around the house again. Behind her she heard the crack of another log splitting. As she unpacked the yarn, figured her yardages and began winding the warp thread around the pegs on the square board, she listened to the steady thwack of Sam's sledgehammer. When the sound ended, she knew that he was gone.

She worked all afternoon, and by suppertime, she'd threaded the loom and woven a few inches of her first napkin. She was excited about the results and longed to run down the tangled path and get Sam to come and see it. But Sam had a date tonight, she reminded herself with a renewed pang of displeasure. He'd asked if his date helped her confusion about him, and she'd said that it did.

She leaned in the doorway of the screened-in back porch and watched the light fade and the tiny indentation that was the beginning of the path disappear.

The oak trees near the woodpile rustled in an evening breeze, and a few yellow leaves floated down onto the freshly chopped wood that Sam had stacked so neatly.

She should be relieved that he had other plans tonight and had left her with no difficult decisions to make. Yet she felt lost and alone. She leaned her forehead against the waffle pattern of the screen and smelled the rusty, metallic scent of the wire. The night was quiet, and although she waited and listened, there was no harmonica music. He would not play for her tonight.

SAM HAD AN ATTACK OF GUILT as he escorted Daphne Michaels to the door of her ranch-style home that night. She'd been a pleasant companion the past few months, but she had one disadvantage—she wasn't Anna. For that he was dumping her, a move that seemed unfair but necessary. On the way home, he'd explained to Daphne that he'd met someone else, and she'd taken the news with grace and style. That made him feel even more guilty.

"Look, I'm sorry that it didn't work out for us," he said, touching her arm.

She put her key into the lock and glanced up at him. "I never did ask who this woman is who has you so mesmerized."

"My—my next-door neighbor."

"Not the one who brought the McCormick place?"

"You know her?"

"My bank arranged for her loan. She's a New Yorker, Sam, through and through. I heard she used to live with a famous New York artist."

"I know about that," he said, and made a conscious effort to unclench his jaw.

"When she was in my office, she was every inch the sophisticated New York designer. I couldn't imagine what she wanted with the McCormick place, although I guess it's chic to have a little country farmhouse these days. But I doubt she'll ever settle permanently in Sumersbury."

Sam had trouble reconciling Daphne's description of a sophisticated New York designer with Anna in a purple sweat suit, carrying one end of his grandmother's loom. "It's a little premature for me to consider anything, anyway," he said, moving away from the door.

"Oh?" She cocked her head. "From the way you announced all of this, I thought you were head over heels in love."

"No," Sam said, trying to be patient. "But the thing is, the possibility's there with Anna. With you and me, Daphne, I don't think the possibility of love was really there, for either of us."

"I never really thought about it," Daphne said, tossing her head as she turned the key in the lock. "I enjoyed having someone to attend concerts with, that's all."

Sam was gentleman enough to let that stand. "So did I, Daphne. Take care." He stepped forward, kissed her lightly on the cheek and headed for his truck.

As he drove home, he wondered if Anna might still be awake. He pictured her seated at his grandmother's loom, and the image brought a tender smile. Later, after he'd changed out of his tuxedo, he sat on his front steps with his harmonica, and deliberately facing in the direction of her house, he played all the songs he knew.

Working the shuttle back and forth in the comforting rhythm that she'd found again so easily, Anna almost didn't hear Sam's harmonica through the barrier of the old house's walls. But she caught a note or two and paused in her work long enough to hear a few more. Grabbing a jacket, she went out to the back porch and sat in a cushioned chair until the concert was over.

He could have been playing for his date, of course, but her instincts said that he wasn't. He was playing for her, and he was alone. Smiling, she walked back into the house and sat at the loom once more. She felt as if Sam had lovingly told her good-night.

ANNA SPENT SUNDAY morning weaving. A pleasant ache in her back and shoulders reminded her of the unaccustomed hours she'd spent at the loom, but the twinge in her muscles also reminded her of accomplishment.

All morning she'd waited for the sound of Sam's truck or his knock at the door if he'd walked over on the path. When noon arrived with still no sign of him, she understood that he was giving her the time and space she'd asked for, and if she was disappointed not to see him once more this weekend, she had only herself to blame.

Back in New York that evening, she gazed at the unadorned walls of her apartment. When Eric had lived with her, the walls had been insufficient to hold the outpouring of his talent. She'd kept the furnishings spare and plain, buying only pieces that wouldn't take attention away from Eric's paintings. Now the paintings were gone, and furniture that had looked spare and plain against the riot of color on his canvases now looked depressingly stark.

The absence of his powerful creativity had been a relief at first. Then, after deciding on the Connecticut farmhouse, she'd had no money for buying new furniture. She could have bought inexpensive prints for the bare walls, yet she hadn't done that, either. Under the pressure of Eric's overwhelming taste, she'd lost track of her own. She could easily take clients' ideas and mold them into a design scheme, but she had avoided choosing a framed print for her own apartment.

She still didn't want to buy art for her walls, she decided, taking furniture catalogs from a bookshelf and settling on the couch with a cup of decaf. She'd rather plan the transformation of Sam's farmhouse. Yet in the next hour, as she leafed through the catalogs and made notes, she kept glancing up at the walls. For the

first time since Eric moved out, she was bothered by
their nakedness.

On Monday, she spent her first break of the day
talking to Vivian, payroll clerk for the department
store and Anna's best friend. Straightforward and as-
sertive, Vivian loved her husband, Jimmy, bright nail
polish and chunky wooden jewelry from South
America. She also loved making people laugh.

"How are things?" Vivian asked when Anna approached her desk with a cup of coffee in one hand.

"Hectic." Anna sat on a chair in front of Vivian's
desk. "Harrison, the guy who won the lottery, wants
his whole house redone in early garish, and it kills me
to spend lots of money on stuff he could pick up at a
discount store. In the meantime, sweet Mrs. Evans
wants imported Oriental carpets and Italian marble
on a budget that wouldn't be enough to refinish this
desk.

"I think you should introduce them and talk them
into switching budgets," Vivian said.

"Now there's an idea."

Vivian's telephone rang. "Excuse me—somebody
probably thinks they ought to get paid around here,"
Vivian said.

Anna sipped her coffee and waited for Vivian to
finish with her caller. Then she put the mug down
and leaned toward Vivian. "I had a specific reason for
coming by," she said, lowering her voice. "Can you
get me a date?"

Vivian's eyes widened and she began to laugh.

"Don't do that, Vivian. Now stop."

"The devil must be freezing his fanny," Vivian said, still grinning. "I believe you said hell would freeze over before you asked me to get you a date."

"So you're going to rub it in, are you? Some friend."

"Do you blame me? You should have heard yourself a couple of months ago. But I thought you'd come around. I am curious, though, as to what brought about the transformation."

"I, um, met this guy over the weekend."

"In your little town of Sumersbury?"

"In my own little neighborhood," Anna said with a smile. "He's my next-door neighbor, and I think I like him a lot."

"I don't get it." Vivian stared at her. "If you've already *met* a guy you like, why do you want another one? Or do you want one for each place so you don't have to cart the same guy back and forth?"

Anna chuckled.

"Well, that could be logical," Vivian said.

"Maybe, but it's not my goal. What I want is another date with a good-looking, intelligent, charming man to find out if the way I reacted to Sam is the way I'd react to any good-looking, intelligent, charming man because I'm lonely and bored." She peered at Vivian. "Did you get that?"

"Just barely. Good thing you're an interior designer and not a newscaster. So you want a test date to find out if you're attracted to men in general these days or this Sam person in particular?"

"Exactly. And because it's a test date, I'd rather it not be with someone from the store. So I thought you could ask Jimmy if one of his single friends might be willing to go out with me."

Vivian rested her chin on her hands. "One of Jimmy's 'good-looking, intelligent, charming' friends? Would you like him to be rich? How about funny? Good at sports, maybe even a former Olympian?"

"You're making fun of me. A passable guy, that's all."

"Will 'passable' be a fair test against your Sam?"

"No."

"Anna, this is a ridiculous thing you want to do, but I'll arrange it, because I'm your friend and I understand that you think you have to do this before you can relax and enjoy Sam."

"Thanks, Vivian." Anna got up and started to leave.

"Friday night?"

Anna stopped. "Well, actually, Thursday might be better."

"Dear one, no man will be complimented if you insist on a Thursday-night date. They'll think you're saving your weekend for others, which you probably are. Friday or Saturday should be the night, unless you want to forget this charade."

"Friday, then." Anna had told Sam that she would

date someone else, and she would do it, by golly—although that meant she couldn't go to Connecticut until Saturday morning.

"I'll let you know when I have something set up," Vivian said, and reached for her telephone.

"Thanks, Viv." Anna smiled her appreciation and left the accounting department. By that afternoon, Vivian had found her a date for Friday night.

Anna spent Monday and Tuesday evenings drawing up recommendations for Sam's house. The combination of planning the rooms in the farmhouse and glancing up to confront her own stark surroundings finally prompted her on Wednesday to buy a print from the store to hang over the couch.

She didn't debate the choice much, and it wasn't until she got the print home that she recognized any significance in what she'd bought. The print was rural, but then she'd always been drawn to farmhouses and barns and vaguely remembered having bought similar scenes before she'd met Eric. Yet none of them had been quite like this one. This picture included children.

She stood with the hammer in her hand and gazed at the print. At last she admitted to herself that it reminded her of Sam. The association could be explained easily: she'd been touched last weekend by what she'd learned about Sam's childhood. But that wasn't all of it. It wasn't a very big leap from Sam as a child to Sam as a father. Instinctively she knew that he longed for that role.

She, on the other hand, had no unfulfilled need to become a mother. At least she didn't think so. Eric certainly hadn't wanted babies around to interfere with his work, and she'd agreed with him that their careers hadn't left room for parenting. But Sam's life, the country life, seemed to beg for the addition of children. Anna decided to give the matter more thought. A lot more thought.

She wished it was Saturday instead of Wednesday and that Sam was next door instead of miles away. The longing to have contact with him grew so strong that she searched for a legitimate reason to call him. Hitting on an idea, she found the notepad where she'd written his number and hurried to the telephone.

"An appointment?" he said after hearing why she'd called. He chuckled in a way that sent warm shivers over her. "What do you need an appointment for? This is Sumersbury, don't forget, not Manhattan."

Anna felt the peace of the country wrap around her at his words and his relaxed tone. "Yes, but some neighbor might have asked for your help again, like last Saturday, and I thought we should have a couple of hours to discuss this without being interrupted," she said, trying to excuse what she realized was an unnecessary call. His silence on the other end made her review what she'd said, and she flushed. "I mean—"

"Anna, if you want two hours of uninterrupted

time with me, you've got it," he said softly. "I'll even take the phone off the hook."

"Oh, Sam, I'm so confused," she admitted, dropping all pretenses. "I called because I miss you."

"That's the best news I've had all day."

"But it doesn't make sense. I don't know you well enough to miss you. I keep wondering if I'm drawn in by everything—the country setting, the loom, the idea of children—"

"The *what*?" Sam choked out.

"Oh, Lord, I didn't mean to say that. Maybe I should hang up now, before I have both feet in my mouth."

"No, wait. I have to hear the explanation for this one."

"I'm babbling, Sam," she said, frantic to cover up her inadvertent slip. "Please forget it. I'm probably working too hard."

"Anna."

"Oh, shoot. It's just that I never thought of being a mother before, and I never bought pictures with children in them. I never bought pictures at all when Eric was here, but he left and took all his pictures, and for months I've had nothing on the walls. But this week the place looked bare, and I finally bought a framed print to hang over the couch, and when I got it home, I realized it had *children* in it." As she paused to take a breath, she heard his gentle laughter. "What's so funny?"

"You make the discovery of children in your picture sound like finding roaches in your cabinets. Don't you like children?"

"Of course I like children, but I've never liked them in my pictures before."

He paused. "Are you trying to say that this picture with children in it has something to do with me?"

"I don't know, " she wailed. "But I hung that thing on the wall, and soon afterward, I made up this dumb excuse to call you. I don't know what any of it means."

"Seems pretty simple to me. City girl with hectic career gazes longingly across the fence to what seems to be peaceful domesticity in the country. I'd like to think I have something to do with your longings, but I may just be convenient."

"Sam, I don't want you ever to 'just be convenient.'"

"We agree on that score. But don't ignore your feelings about possibly changing your life-style. You can do that whether I'm part of the change or not."

"I know. It's just—Anyway, I have a date for Friday night."

"Whoopee."

"You suggested it."

"So I did." He sighed. "Is he a wonderful guy?"

"We'll see."

"Will you tell me how the date goes? I need to get a fix on our situation, too."

"I'll tell you. Are you free at ten on Saturday morning?"

"I'm free anytime you're in Sumersbury."

"You weren't last Saturday night," she chided.

"Temporarily I wasn't, you're right. But that's— Well, never mind. So you won't be coming up on Friday night this week?"

"No. I'll be seeing a musical with Ted."

"I used to like the name Ted."

"Do you think I should cancel this date?" she asked, almost wishing he'd say yes.

"I guess not. If you go and have a wonderful time, we'll both have a better idea where we stand."

"And if I have a lousy time?"

He laughed in that warm way that she'd come to treasure. "Then my prayers will be answered."

6

ANNA ARRIVED IN SUMERSBURY by nine-thirty. She walked through the front door and put her sack of groceries down on the parlor floor. "Hello, loom," she said, walking over to touch the sun-warmed wood. Her fingers left faint prints in a week's worth of dust. If she was here every day, the loom wouldn't get this dusty. But she wasn't here every day.

For a minute she allowed herself the fantasy of living in this house permanently. Unfortunately she'd have nothing to live *on*. Other than interior design, she had no marketable skills. She couldn't even type very well. And supposing that she'd be lucky enough to find some minimum-wage job in Sumersbury, that income wouldn't begin to make payments on this house.

Of course, if she married someone like Sam... She brought her thoughts up short and rebuked herself for even thinking such a thing. She'd always believed a woman should pull her financial weight in a relationship. She'd insisted on that with Eric, and her decision had proved wise.

Anna glanced at her watch and picked up the grocery sack. She had just enough time to put away her food and drive over to Sam's. She'd made an appointment, and she intended to be a little early. After refrigerating the perishables and shoving the rest into cupboards, Anna walked out to the car, where she'd left her catalogs, notes and a few rough sketches.

Halfway into the driver's seat, she changed her mind and gathered up her materials. Locking the car, she walked around the house and across the leaf-strewn yard. With the distinctive outcropping of granite to guide her, she located the narrow pathway through the woods. Feeling a little like Davy Crockett or Daniel Boone, she stepped from the sunny clearing into the shade of the trees.

Picking her way up the gradual ascent of the trail propelled her back to childhood memories of hide-and-seek, cowboys and Indians and special places that only best friends knew about. Maybe her nose triggered her imagination, she thought, as it identified the toasted smell of dry leaves in a patch of sun and the moist richness of wet bark. Little brown birds—sparrows or finches, she decided—fluttered through branches of partially denuded trees and snatched a few remaining berries from bushes. For them the banquet was nearly over, and they'd have to fly south very soon.

A chipmunk scampered across the path, and with a flick of its tail, disappeared in a rustle of underbrush. Anna stopped and tried to figure out where the little animal had gone, but the camouflage was too perfect. She wondered what wildlife she'd see if she sat on a nearby fallen log and waited, especially at dusk. Perhaps a deer or a raccoon.

Thinking of raccoons reminded her of Estelle's singing, which reminded her of Sam and her appointment. Anna laughed and continued along the path. She couldn't sit on any logs today, or she'd be late. Besides, the prospect of being with Sam outweighed her interest in wildlife. It would be nice, though, to have the leisure to be with Sam *and* sit on the log. Had she known about the path before, she might have explored it this summer.

No, you wouldn't have, contradicted a voice within her. *You were pulled inside yourself like a hermit crab in its borrowed shell. You weren't into exploring anything.* But through luck or fate, she'd been ready to emerge from her shell when the opportunity presented itself through a television special, a loom and a man.

She still wasn't clear where her new directions would lead, but life was interesting and fun again. New possibilities, including the exploration of this lovely path, seemed to appear with each day. She hurried forward as the trail dipped toward Sam's farmhouse.

A few hundred yards from his house, the overgrown charm of the woods gave way to precise rows of evergreens. The path had been allowed to continue its meandering route, marked by occasional stones placed along each side. Wherever the trail crossed a line of trees, a space had been left unplanted. Whether credit for preserving the original historic path belonged to Sam or his grandfather, Anna approved of the decision.

The path ended in Sam's backyard. The barn was to her left, and a low rock wall bordered the other side of his property. His small back porch, not screened as hers was, lay directly in front of her. She noticed an old, unused horseshoes pit and a stack of firewood much larger than hers.

Several pastel-colored dish towels flapped like semaphore flags on a clothesline that sagged in the middle. She walked over to the line and examined one of the towels. Sure enough, it was handwoven. Just as Sam had told her, he used his grandmother's handiwork to accomplish mundane chores, as his grandmother would have wanted.

The towels were dry. Anna put down her stack of materials on the brown grass at her feet and removed the first clothespin, the old-fashioned kind that looked like an armless human figure. Anna remembered using bits of cloth and a little paint to transform clothespins like this into dolls. She found the clothespin holder hanging on the next line and tossed the pin inside. Then she removed the next pin, folded the towel and put it on top of her notes.

In a few minutes she knocked on Sam's back door.

He opened it and gave her a smile of pleased surprise. "I was listening for your car, but—"

"But I came over on the path," she said. "And I'm late, but I stopped to bring in your dish towels." She held out the folded stack resting on top of her bundle of paper and catalogs.

"Why, thanks." He laughed and took the dish towels while he ushered her into the kitchen. "But you really didn't have to take care of my laundry."

"I know. I wanted to. Wooden clothespins, hand-woven towels drying on a backyard line—you can't imagine what a treat that is for a city girl. Too bad the TV people will be here in the dead of winter, and you can't have the towels hanging out for the cameras."

"You're teasing me," he said as he put the stack on a butcher-block counter.

"Believe it or not," she said, gazing at him and absorbing the comfort of his presence, "I'm not kidding. I had fun taking down the wash. Do you dry all your laundry that way, on the line?"

"Sorry to disappoint you, but no. I have an automatic dryer like everyone else, but with the dish towels I just—" He shrugged. "I like hanging them out."

"And taking them in? I didn't spoil your fun, did I?"

He grinned. "Even if you did, I'd be a mean man to deny you the thrill you just had. You're welcome to commune with that clothesline anytime."

"Now *you're* making fun of *me*."

"I wouldn't dare. I've admitted hanging those towels out for no good reason, so I guess we're both touched in the head."

Anna laughed. "I'll buy that."

"God, it's good to see you again."

His comment faded her smile, changed the mood. She hugged her bundle of materials against her chest.

"Now I've scared you," he said.

"A little."

"Come on," he said, sweeping his arm toward the parlor. "I've cleaned my ledgers off the sofa. We can sit there and go over what you've brought. I'll be good. I promise. I won't ask about your date last night until we're finished, even if the need to know is burning through me like hot coals. I'll probably fidget some, but disregard any signs of my discomfort. It will pass."

She chuckled. "Oh, Sam."

"Can't help it, Anna. But we really should decide about the house stuff first, or we may never get to it. From that stack of material you have, I figure you've worked pretty hard on this project."

"I want to do a good job."

"And I'm sure you will. Speaking of that, would you like to see how the hall looks without the wallpaper?"

"You've taken it off already?" She'd expected to have to prod him on that unpleasant job.

"All gone. I'll show you."

She followed him through the dining room into the parlor and up the stairs. "My goodness," she said, blinking at the white walls running the length of the hall. "What a difference."

Sam stuck his hands into the back pockets of his jeans and looked pleased with himself. "I had to pick the shade of white to use, but we could paint another shade over this if you don't like it. I never knew there were so many different whites in the paint world."

Anna evaluated the look of the hall. "I think this is perfect," she said, and enjoyed his smile of satisfaction. "All it needs is some stenciling along the top, near the ceiling."

"Stenciling, like we did in grade school?"

"Essentially. I brought some patterns for you to look at. Painting in the outlines of a stencil takes more patience than skill."

"I don't have a real good supply of either."

She glanced at him. "Judging from this hallway, I doubt that. After taking off wallpaper, you'll think stenciling is wonderful fun. Besides, it's very 'in' right now. The TV people will be delighted, and with both of us working, the job shouldn't take very—"

"You'll help?"

"Sure. I told you it was kind of fun."

Sam shook his head and looked bewildered. "But you're the designer. You're not supposed to be involved with the dirty work, are you?"

"Not in the designing I do for the store. You're right about that. If someone wants stenciling, I have it done and the store gets a percentage. But this isn't a job for the store, although I may end up buying a few things there." She paused. "You know, maybe that's part of what's been missing from my work. Maybe I have this thing for manual labor," she added, chuckling at herself. "After all, I felt compelled to fold your dish towels, and now I'm all excited about stenciling designs on your walls. Maybe we should continue the pattern into the parlor, too."

"Lady, if you crave manual labor, you'd better move to the country. I'll put you to work on the Christmas trees."

"Now let's not get carried away. I don't want to become a farm worker, but the satisfaction of doing things with my hands..." She gazed off into space as the concept settled into her mind. No wonder she'd been drawn to the loom.

"I wish you hadn't phrased it quite that way."

She glanced at Sam. "What?"

"I'm trying so hard not to kiss you, and you want to talk about doing things with your hands."

She flushed as her heartbeat quickened. "Sam, I didn't intend to—"

"I know," he said with a gentle look. "Never mind. I think we ought to go downstairs and see what you've dreamed up for the rest of the house." He turned and led the way to the sofa in the parlor.

She followed, her stomach churning at his open admission that he wanted her. No matter how much she tried to tamp down her emotions, Sam kept stirring them up again. Yet her fear of abandoning herself to her feelings still outweighed the lure of Sam's kisses. She didn't trust an attraction that had taken hold so quickly.

They sat on the sofa a cushion width apart, and Anna placed her materials deliberately between them. "Okay," she began, "let's start with what we're sitting on."

"Meaning the sofa, of course," he interjected with a wink.

"Now, Sam, if you're going to sabotage—"

"Sorry."

With a look of warning that made him chuckle, she started over. "I'd like to have the sofa recovered in this fabric," she said, rummaging through her fabric swatches and holding up a small red print.

"Bright."

"Yes. This room needs stronger contrasts to pick up the colors of the braided rug. Plus, the red will make a perfect backdrop for your grandmother's hand-woven cushions. The print is small enough that it won't clash with the patterns in the pillows."

"If you say so."

"And the curtains should come down. I'd like the windows bare, if you can stand it."

"Bare windows?" Sam looked doubtful.

"Yes," she said, warming with enthusiasm. "Let the sun stream in. I noticed a whole collection of ruby glassware in the kitchen. We can set some on the windowsill and more on the mantel, once it's cleared and polished. The sun coming through that red glass will make the whole room glow." The doubt eased from his expression, but she didn't want to force anything on him. "Listen, if you really hate anything I suggest, speak up."

"Go on."

"Well..." She hesitated. "I think you should store those two armchairs and buy new ones. That may be your biggest expense, but if we cut corners in other areas, the new chairs will fit into the budget you gave me."

"Would you like to keep them at your house? You're a little short on furniture over there."

"Um, temporarily," she said, not wanting to tell him how much she despised the chairs. They might have been favorites of his grandparents, placed as they were flanking the fireplace.

"You don't like them at all, do you?"

Anna sighed. "I don't want to attack any memories, but I'd recommend donating those chairs to the next church rummage sale."

He rubbed his chin and gazed at her. At last he smiled. "That wasn't easy to say, was it?"

Anna shook her head.

"What if I insisted on keeping those chairs in the room?"

Anna shrugged. "We'd have them reupholstered and hope for the best, but I figure anyone who hires me deserves my honest opinion."

"I appreciate that," he said, his gaze warm. "More than you know. The chairs go."

Anna sighed with relief and hurried on. "Here's what I recommend for a replacement," she said, opening a catalog to a page full of chairs. "In white leather."

"Wow."

"I know. Most people aren't used to spending that kind of money, but the chairs could last you a lifetime, Sam."

"Me and someone else," he said. "I can't very well sit in both of them at once." He glanced up from the page. "Have you ever tried one of these? Are they comfortable?"

"There's a floor model in the store, and I stop to relax in it every time I go by, if I can."

"Then you like these chairs, too?"

"Yes," she said, aware of the overtones of their conversation.

"Good. Oh, by the way, Tom from the hardware store has already picked up the sleigh bed and chest to refinish. He said about a week."

"You've been busy," she said, closing the catalog and trying to think of the sleigh bed as a designer would and not the way a woman would.

"Not busy enough, unfortunately."

She decided to ignore that remark. "Now, the coffee table and end tables will be fine as is, with a good beeswax polishing, but I'd like to suggest we replace the lamps with some that I found." She opened another catalog and spread it out between them.

"Fine," he said without looking at the page.

"You don't even know which ones I'm talking about," she said, her hand trembling a little as she absorbed the intensity of his gaze. "I marked them. One is a floor model and the others are—"

"Tell me about your date last night."

"I thought that we agreed that the design project was more—"

"Please. Tell me if you had a wonderful time, and if you did, we'll continue with this decorating chitchat. I have to know, that's all."

"And...what if I didn't have a wonderful time?" she asked, her heart racing.

His smile began with his eyes. "You didn't?"

"Not very," she said around the dryness in her throat.

"But he was a real nerd, right? Either skinny as a bean pole or too fat, and his conversation was boring, right?"

Anna shook her head. "No. Ted's very nice looking, and we had no trouble talking to each other. But..."

Sam closed the catalog of lamps. Then he picked up the stack of materials that separated him from Anna and laid them on the coffee table. "Go on," he said, moving next to her and putting his arm along the back of the sofa.

"Sam, we haven't finished what we set out to do."

"That's okay. I'm the client, and what you're explaining is far more interesting to me right now than lamps. What about this Ted guy? What comes after the sentence that began with 'but'?"

She twisted her hands and glanced at him. "He didn't make me feel..."

"The way you do now?" he said softly.

"Sam, I don't know what this is, this craziness between you and me. I don't trust it."

"I know." His gaze was understanding as he ran his finger along the curve of her jaw. "But you're not going to trust anything you run away from."

"Sam, what if you were right about being the convenient man in my country idyll? What if it's the setting, the clothesline, the lovely path between our houses that makes me feel this way?"

He continued to explore the planes of her face, tracing her cheekbones and her eyebrows. "Want me to move to the city so you can find out if the attraction is regional?" His gentle exploration gave her goose bumps.

"No," she said, gazing into his very blue eyes. "I want... I think I want you to kiss me."

The corners of his mouth turned up. "But you're not sure."

She let out her breath slowly. "Maybe it won't be like last time, and then I'll know the harmonica music had something to do with everything."

"Maybe." He cupped her face and leaned closer.

"And last time I'd had some wine, and I was a little tired and more susceptible..."

He tipped her mouth toward his and stroked her bottom lip with his thumb, exerting gentle pressure to relax her jaw. "Do you think you've analyzed this enough, or do you have more to say on the subject?"

"This is very unprofessional, Sam," she said halfheartedly.

"Don't go passing judgment until I'm finished," he murmured, his breath warm on her face.

"No, I meant that—"

"Anna, you talk too much." His mouth settled against hers with gentle sureness.

Ignition, she thought as her body responded and logic fell away like the platform of a launched rocket. *Oh, Sam.* She reached for his shoulders and held on as the seductive process began. She waited, trembling, as he guided her backward until her head rested against his outstretched arm. When he lifted his lips from hers, it was only to return with greater purpose. Gradually he probed deeper, asked for more. She gave it.

She didn't realize she'd arched her back and thrust her breasts forward until he touched her there. Her heartbeat thundered in her ears, but she didn't—couldn't—stop his knowing caress. The pleasure was too exquisite. He drew down the zipper of her sweat jacket with measured slowness, giving her all the chances she needed to stop his hand, to signal her limits.

She allowed the jacket to fall open, allowed him to unfasten the front clasp of her bra and moaned with excitement when his callused hand stroked her hot skin. The force of their kiss had become so great that when he lifted his head, she was gasping.

"If you don't stop this, I'll probably make love to you right here on this sofa," he said, breathing hard himself. "Would you rather go upstairs?"

She closed her eyes and fought for breath. "Sam, I don't—"

"That's why I'm asking. Talk to me, Anna."

She looked into his face, and the fierce desire there took her breath away once more. "Not yet," she managed to say, wondering if she meant it. "Not yet, Sam." She watched him struggle to master his emotions. "I stopped thinking just now," she said. "And I wanted everything you were giving me. Maybe if you'd kept on without asking, I would have..."

"But that's no good. If it happens, I want it to be your choice. Knowing all the reservations you've had about us, I had to ask. I don't want regrets afterward."

"Nor do I," she said softly, touching his cheek. "Thanks, Sam."

He turned his head to kiss her palm. Then he glanced down at her uncovered breasts, where his hand still rested. "You're beautiful," he said. "Simply beautiful." Without warning, he cupped her fullness and leaned down to kiss one dusky tip.

She caught her breath as sensation flowed from where he'd kissed her and pooled in the heated center of her body.

"I'm not trying to change your mind," he said, and released her so that he could refasten her bra. "Because I won't do that. I was just expressing my appreciation." He zipped up her jacket and looked into her eyes. "And I'll make you a promise. If you do decide that we'll make love, whenever that is, we'll have one hell of a time."

She smiled. "And how can you be sure?"

"I have some basis of comparison, too, you know."

She thought about last Saturday night. "Did you come home early from that date you had?" she asked, made bolder by what they'd just shared.

"Yes."

"Why?"

He grinned. "I've decided to save myself for you."

"Oh, Sam! You're teasing me again."

"Actually, I'm not. I realized sometime during the evening with Daphne—"

"I used to like the name Daphne," she interrupted.

"Are you jealous? That's great!"

"Never mind that. What did you realize?"

"That I'd kissed you once, and I'd kissed Daphne, oh, maybe a hund—"

"Skip the details, please."

His grin became broader. "Okay. Anyway, that one kiss with you packed more wallop than any number of kisses I'd shared with Daphne. You spoiled me for her, is what it amounts to."

"What a shame. By the way, she wouldn't be the branch manager for the bank, would she?"

"That's her."

"I'm complimented. I remember her from when I took out my loan. She's a very attractive woman."

"She remembers you, too."

"You told her about me?"

He shrugged. "I had to offer some explanation for ending our relationship, so I mentioned I'd met someone else. She asked who, and when I said you were my next-door neighbor, she knew who you were."

"Small towns," Anna said, shaking her head.

"She also said that you were a dyed-in-the-wool New Yorker who would never settle in Sumersbury in a million years."

Anna gazed up at him, and the silence lengthened. "What if she turns out to be right?"

He held her gaze with compelling force. "And what if she turns out to be wrong?"

7

ANNA HAD TO ADMIRE Sam's self-control. He made no more attempts to persuade her into bed while they selected lamps for the parlor and picked a pinecone pattern for the stenciling in the hall. He also accepted her recommendations for reupholstering the chair and ottoman in the master bedroom.

"I want to use that woven blanket your grandmother made as an accent, possibly thrown over the chair as you, in fact, do," Anna said. "And the other thing I'd really like for that room is a quilt. Antique would be nice, but you don't have any of those, do you?"

"Nope. Quilts weren't my grandmother's thing, but I'll bet Tessie can steer you in the right direction on that."

"The quilt might be our only other big expense," Anna warned. "Handmade quilts aren't cheap."

"I suppose not, but I've always wanted one, now that you mention it. I could consider it my Christmas present to myself."

"Then you'd better be in on buying it."

"You bet. Get Tessie to give you some names of

women who sew and sell quilts, and we'll set aside a Saturday afternoon to go looking. It'll be fun."

"I think you're right about that," Anna said, enjoying the easy tone they could manage with each other, even after such a steamy scene had taken place between them. She wondered if that meant she and Sam could be friends, as well as lovers. "I also think we've made enough crucial decisions for now. Once the basics are in place, we'll plan Christmas decorations. Considering what you sell, I'd recommend a tree in every room, for starters."

Sam laughed. "That I can do."

"I'd also like to use some of the old toys in your cubbyhole as accents. Could we do that?"

"We're going to really hit the nostalgia, right?"

"I think that's what they want, from what you..." She paused as his telephone rang. When he didn't get up to answer it, she glanced at him questioningly.

"You said two hours of uninterrupted time," he said. "Two hours isn't up yet."

"Maybe not, but ringing telephones drive me crazy."

"I knew I should have taken it off the hook," he said, pushing himself up with a sigh. "But I know who it is, and she can wait."

"She?"

"Estelle Terwiliger." He walked without haste to the wall telephone in the kitchen. In a few minutes he was back, his expression resigned. "Now she wants a pond. A frozen pond. With skaters. It's not bad enough that she wants to drag the Bentson kids' pet doe into it and make the poor animal wear a set of antlers, but—"

"Antlers? I don't—"

"A reindeer," Sam explained in a toneless voice, slumping onto the sofa. "She wants the TV people to get a shot of Santa in his sleigh jingling through the snowy streets of Sumersbury. She plans to tell them we have a tradition of doing that. She's got the Bentson kids teaching their doe to pull a wagon, so it'll get used to a harness. Lord knows where she'll find a sleigh."

"Don't let her put runners on your bed."

"Don't worry."

He looked so dark and forbidding that Anna chuckled. "I'm sorry. I'm sure all of this isn't funny to you. Does Estelle call often?"

"Every day. The town choir is a reality, and I think she's abandoned the organ for a town orchestra. That's where the pond and skaters come in."

"The orchestra will be on skates?"

Sam glanced up and began chuckling with her. "Not yet. But give Estelle time and she'll think of that, too. As it stands now, the orchestra will play 'The Skaters' Waltz' beside the pond, which doesn't even exist yet, by the way. Then, assuming that a pond exists and the weather cooperates and freezes it solid, costumed skaters will whirl around in time to the music. This also is being billed as a town tradition."

"Does Sumersbury *have* any holiday traditions, other than what Estelle is dreaming up?"

Sam rubbed his chin. "Let's see. The day after Thanksgiving we put a few scraggly decorations on the lampposts lining the main street. I usually help with that, and I've been meaning to suggest that we take up a collection from the merchants for new decorations. Now I'll leave that to Estelle. She'll probably raise money to string the whole town with colored lights."

"That's it, then, a few decorations?"

"The churches each have special services, but yeah, that's about it, except for Edgar Madison, who starts drinking on Thanksgiving and can be seen staggering around most of December."

"I'm beginning to see why Estelle's creating traditions. She wants Sumersbury to look good. Don't forget that you started this with your suggestion of a town choir."

"I did...I did," Sam muttered, leaning his head back and closing his eyes. "And I can already see that I'll live to regret it. A frozen pond? We may not have snow, for Pete's sake! Then what'll she expect—an army of people with Ivory Snow? I really—Oh, Lord, there's the phone again. I'm not going to answer."

"Has Estelle ever called twice in one day?"

"No, but it's not too late for her to start. Do you realize this is only September? We have more than two months to go!"

"Sam, please answer the phone."

He opened his eyes. "Don't you ever let yours ring?"

"No."

"Sometimes, in a small town, you have to," he said, but he stood and walked back to the kitchen once more. This time, when he returned and sat beside her, his expression was impatient.

"Estelle again?"

"No. Worse."

"After the way you've been complaining, I can't imagine anyone worse."

"That's because you don't know my mother."

Anna sat up straighter. "Your mother just called?"

"Yep." He looked at her. "She's heard about my great honor and the TV special. She wants to come down from Boston and be here. What she wants," he said, rubbing a hand over his face, "is to be on television. Lord help us."

Anna moved closer and put her hand on his shoulder. "It doesn't seem right, does it? You achieve something and everyone wants a ride on the bandwagon."

"Everyone but you," he said, smiling at her. "I'll bet you'd rather be out of town that weekend."

"Truthfully, yes."

"I'd appreciate it if you'd stay and face the music with me, Anna."

"You mean 'The Skaters' Waltz,' the 'Hallelujah Chorus' and the 'Ave Maria'? That music?"

He laughed. "That music."

"Sure," she agreed, unable to deny him her support. "I'll be here."

"Thanks." He gazed into her eyes. "It's a date."

She felt the tug of passion begin, and she looked away. "In the meantime, I'll see Tessie this afternoon about the quilt. I want to consult with her about the next stage of my weaving, too."

"How's that coming along?"

"Great. I'm planning something for a client, a sweet lady with champagne tastes and a beer budget. She wants a handwoven dresser scarf, and I know exactly the kind she means. I could make it for half the cost of buying it in a New York shop and charge her a little over my cost."

"Don't shortchange yourself," Sam warned. "Get fair value for your work."

"I'm not going to worry about that right now," she countered, ignoring his frown. "It would be fun for me and provide her with exactly what she needs at a price she can afford. My enjoyment will be part of my fee."

"If you say so."

"Sam, you of all people should understand. Didn't you lecture me once about neighborliness?"

His face relaxed. "You're right. And my grandmother used to sell things far under their value, too. But I always thought she could have made a tidy sum with her weaving, if she'd tried."

"Maybe that would have taken the joy out, to weave for a living."

"Maybe."

Anna gathered her materials. "I've got to go."

"Want a lift?" he asked as they both stood.

"That's okay. I loved walking over on the path. I'll just go back that way."

"I'll be glad to walk you home."

"Thanks, but we both have things to do." As they entered the kitchen, the telephone began ringing again. "Especially you," she said.

"That darn thing. I'd love to take it out."

"Sam, you're a businessman. You're an accountant and a tree salesman, so you'd better answer your calls. This hectic period will be over before you know it. See you later," she called, and walked out the back door into the sunshine. Behind her, she heard him sigh and pick up the phone.

On the walk back home, she realized that he hadn't arranged to see her again this weekend to discuss the design project, and they'd made no social arrangements, either. Just as well, she decided. She needed time to weave and collect her thoughts. The two activities went well together.

After a quick tuna sandwich, Anna drove to town and parked in front of Tessie's yarn shop. She found Tessie with two gray-haired customers who were debating the instructions of a knitting pattern and the right size of needles.

When the bell hanging over the door jingled, Tessie looked toward the door and smiled. "Hello, Anna. Be with you in a minute."

Both of her customers made quarter turns that gave them a quick glimpse of who had come through the door. Anna nodded once and walked over to a revolving rack of knitting, weaving and crocheting magazines. After a moment, the taller of the two women joined her by the rack of magazines, pulled out a few, scanned the covers and put them back.

Anna found a weaving magazine and flipped through it.

"You interested in weaving?" asked the woman, glancing at the magazine in Anna's hand.

"Yes." Anna gave her a quick smile and returned to her reading.

"Got a loom?"

"Um, I—yes."

"You wouldn't be Anna Tilford, by any chance?"

Anna glanced up briefly. "Yes, I am."

"Heard you borrowed Hilary Schute's loom. Estelle told me. Hilary was a wonderful weaver. I bought some of her dish towels at a craft fair put on by the guild. Have them still."

"That's nice." Anna made just enough eye contact to be polite, but she continued to scan the page in front of her.

"I used to buy some of Hilary's work for gifts, too. Will you be weaving anything to sell?"

"Well, I—"

"Anna's only getting started," Tessie cut in. She rang up the women's purchases and whipped around the counter in a seeming rescue attempt. "She probably doesn't know what she's planning to do with her work."

"That's fine," the tall woman said, smiling, "but I'm surprised Estelle hasn't asked you to join the guild. She must be too busy with this Christmas thing. We'd love to have you, in any case. Tessie here hardly ever makes meetings anymore, and I can't seem to talk her into weaving projects to sell, either."

"I really am a beginner," Anna said, trying to imagine herself joining the Sumersbury Craft Guild. No way.

"All levels of craft ability are welcome," the woman said as her shorter friend came to stand beside her. "Right, Emma?"

"You bet," the shorter woman said. "We're a charity group, you see. We make things and sell them at craft fairs. Part of the money goes to the woman who made the item and part to our fund for good causes."

"Which this year," the taller woman said, "will be all the preparations for the TV special."

"I imagine you're excited about that, being next door to Sam and all," Emma said. "And with you redecorating Sam's house."

"It is exciting," Anna admitted, holding back a smile as she thought of the scene on the sofa not long ago.

"We'd best be toddling along, Emma," the taller woman said. "And goodness, I've forgotten my manners. I'm Lettie Godwin, and this here's Emma Simpson. Call us if you need help or have questions about the guild. We'd be pleased to have you join."

"Thank you," Anna said, "I'll keep that in mind."

After the women left, Tessie gave her a sheepish look. "Sorry about that. But this TV special and now your part in it have been the talk of the town. Not much goes on in Sumersbury, and this is more excitement than we've had since the Christmas Edgar Madison took the pledge and spent the first week of December sober."

Anna laughed. "I've apparently been the talk of the town before this all happened. Little did I realize I was routinely discussed as 'that city woman who bought the McCormick place.'"

"Yes, you were." Tessie's eyes twinkled.

"Listen, before I ask you my weaving questions, there's one thing I can't forget. I need a handmade quilt for Sam's sleigh bed, and the name of someone who has them to sell or can make one up to order. Any suggestions?"

"You may not like my suggestion."

"Why?"

"Because the best person to contact about that is the president of the Sumersbury Craft Guild."

Anna rolled her eyes. "Estelle Terwiliger."

"The same. But honestly, she knows who is making quilts. Because quilts don't use yarn, I'm not privy to that information, generally."

"I guess I hoped you could be my contact point for all that sort of thing. I also need a sofa, a chair and an ottoman reupholstered. I'll provide the material, but I hate to ship the pieces all the way to New York to have them done."

"Now that I can help you with," Tessie said. "I have a good friend who does that. Let me get his card."

As Tessie hurried to the back of the shop, Anna rested one hip against the counter and gazed at the bins of colored yarns. Soon she'd picked the ones she'd use for her client's dresser scarf. She was discovering that there was a market for handwoven goods. Sam's grandmother might have been able to bring in quite a bit of money with her work, if she'd been so inclined. Anna filed the information away to think about later, among other things, while she was weaving.

By the time she left Tessie's shop, the sun had disappeared behind a growing bank of flannel-gray clouds, and the temperature had dropped several degrees. Anna stopped by the Sumersbury grocery for tea bags and a package of Pepperidge Farm cookies. The weather was turning just right for a cozy fire, tea and cookies and her weaving.

Late afternoon found her with a good start on her client's dresser scarf, a delicate weave of mauves and pinks that would combine perfectly with the woman's Victorian bedroom decor. Anna got up from the bench to stretch and bring in more logs for the fire. She'd eaten cookies and drunk tea all afternoon, and she didn't feel like cooking dinner.

She grabbed her jacket from the hook by the back door and went out through the porch to the yard. Dusk had come earlier than usual because of the clouds, and a cool, moist breeze blew her unzipped jacket open. She zipped it and walked toward the woodpile.

As she approached, a gray squirrel scampered away from its perch on top of the stacked logs. Anna wished it would come back. Her quiet afternoon of weaving had convinced her that she'd be very happy to spend winter weekends like this. The peaceful setting, the soothing repetition of the shuttle and beater bar and the crackling heat of the fire all satisfied her enormously. But she was having a small problem with solitude.

Maybe a big problem, she acknowledged as she piled three medium-size pieces of wood in the crook of her arm and returned to the house. She kept expecting Sam to contact her, but her phone was silent and her driveway empty. He'd said he wanted her, kissed her passionately, then left her alone.

Anna realized that she was being perverse; she'd asked him to back off. Now she wished he hadn't been so willing to take her suggestion. From the looks of things, she'd spend the rest of the weekend alone with her weaving.

"Well, phooey," she muttered, and took the wood inside to stack it on the hearth. Then she went back for another load, figuring she might as well stock up and not have to stumble around out here in the dark for more wood. She had a flashlight, but the beam was weak. On her way back in, she cocked her head and listened for Sam's harmonica. Nothing. With a sigh she carried her bundle inside.

As the countryside grew dark outside her windows, Anna built up the fire and sat on the floor in front of it. She should have accepted the loan of Sam's awful chairs, she thought, chuckling at herself. She'd spent her summer weekends out on the back porch, reading and thinking. The lack of furniture in the house hadn't bothered her then.

At last, when her fanny got sore from sitting on the pine floor, she got up and trudged out to the back porch. A cushioned metal porch chair was better than a hard backed dining room chair, she concluded, maneuvering the thing through the kitchen and around the table in the dining room.

Once the chair was in place, she decided a glass of wine was in order, and she returned to the kitchen and poured some. Settled at last in her porch chair, she held up her glass of Burgundy and enjoyed the flicker of flames through the rose-red wine. "Here's to you, Sam," she murmured, and took a generous sip.

She leaned back and congratulated herself on the excellent fire she'd built, for a city girl. She'd learned the technique one Christmas when her parents had rented a place in the country and organized a big family reunion. Anna hadn't thought about that Christmas in years, but she wondered if perhaps that isolated experience had created her nostalgia for this kind of life.

Whatever drove her, she needed this setting and hoped to keep it part of her life. Sam felt the same way, and that enhanced his appeal. Sam. What was he doing tonight? In only a short time she'd returned to thoughts of him. He hadn't serenaded her with his harmonica, or if he had, the breeze had blown the notes away.

Maybe he wasn't even home, she thought. He could be on a date. That prospect was so unsettling that Anna got out of her chair and began to pace with her wineglass. He'd talked about an active social life, and so what if he'd dropped off last Saturday's companion early? Tonight he might have someone more interesting to be with, to talk with, to hold hands and—Anna clenched her teeth. Damn, but she hated the thought of Sam kissing someone else...or more. She had no claims on him.

Or he might be home alone, just as she was. He might be working on his accounting business, she thought with an indulgent smile. He could be catching up on work so that he'd have more free time next weekend.

But which was it? The need to know became more urgent with every length of the room Anna covered. She could call, of course, or simply drive over, but that could prove embarrassing if he happened to be at the house with another woman.

There was, of course, the path.

At first Anna dismissed the idea of taking the path over to Sam's. She'd have to live with not knowing his whereabouts tonight. She'd stop drinking wine in front of the fireplace and start weaving again to take her mind off Sam.

But she'd been across the path twice that day...

However, both times had been in broad daylight, and the woods would be dark and tricky at night. No telling what could happen to her running around in the dark like that.

But she had a flashlight...

So what if she made it through the woods with her weak little flashlight? What on earth did she plan to do, sneak over and spy on him? Was she thinking about creeping up behind his house and checking for lights, or seeing if his truck was there, and if it was, listening for the sound of a female voice?

Exactly.

Anna began to giggle and wondered if half a glass of wine had affected her reasoning. Taking the path over to Sam's now seemed like a daring adventure, the sort of zany thing she hadn't done enough of in her life. All things considered, it was a fairly safe adventure. She had a flashlight and she knew the way. The worst thing she might run into would be a frightened skunk. Besides, as a young girl she'd always wanted to be like Nancy Drew, the supersleuth of her favorite mysteries.

Anna put the screen in front of the fire, which had settled into a steady flame that no longer crackled and spit. She pulled the porch chair out of range, just in case, but the hearth was wide, and she wouldn't be gone very long. She put her half-full wineglass on the hearth and went out to the kitchen.

Pulling on her jacket again and taking the flashlight from a drawer, she went out through the porch, leaving the doors open. Sam left his house unlocked all the time, she'd noticed, and she'd be back before long, anyway.

Once she'd moved out of the light from her kitchen window, she realized how very black the night was in the country, especially with clouds hiding the stars. She switched on her flashlight and beamed it around the backyard until it bounced off the gray outcropping of rocks that marked the beginning of the path. With a shiver of excitement, she started toward it.

8

A SHORT DISTANCE AWAY, in the kitchen of his farm-house, Sam stood in front of an open refrigerator door and tried to work up some enthusiasm for making dinner. He hadn't been able to get excited about much of anything all afternoon. Even his harmonica hadn't interested him, because playing it only reminded him that Anna was in her house and he was in his.

He stared at the food illuminated by the ghostly light inside the refrigerator. Some leftover ham, a few eggs—he could make an omelet. He could make two omelets and offer one to Anna, assuming she hadn't eaten. He should also forget that idea. She needed time and he would give her time.

He took out the ham and put it back. Hot dogs. That would be easy. Hell, he wasn't even hungry. Should he call her, find out if she'd eaten dinner? Wasn't it pretty stupid for them to each eat alone when they were neighbors for Pete's sake?

Sam pictured her weaving all afternoon, forgetting about food until her stomach began to growl. His grandmother had been like that, so absorbed in her work that everything else faded away. He still hadn't seen what Anna was making. If he drove over and invited her in person, he could take a look at what was on the loom. Then, if she didn't want to share supper with him, he'd simply admire her work and leave.

Either way he'd at least get to *see* her once more before she went back to New York. If he called, she might reject him, and he'd have to wait until next weekend, when the work on the house would give them no choice but to interact. He'd drive over.

Grabbing his jacket, he went out the front door and hopped into the truck. As he backed around and headed down the driveway, he switched on the wipers to clear the windshield of a slight, drizzling rain. If Anna agreed to have supper with him, he'd build a fire tonight. He'd stored some wood under the back porch, and it would be dry.

He parked in her driveway beside her car and hurried up to the door. He smelled the smoke from her chimney and wondered if he'd be able to lure her out into a rainy night when she'd already made herself a warm fire. But then he shouldn't rule out the possibility that she'd ask him to stay and eat with her. He rapped on the door a second time.

While waiting for her to answer, he moved around restlessly under the shelter of the front overhang. What would he say? That his grandmother used to forget to eat while she was weaving, and he was here to offer support?

Yeah, he'd say that. Sounded as good as anything. He couldn't very well tell her that he hadn't been able to stay away, despite all his best intentions. But why on earth was it taking her so long to answer the door? He pounded louder and waited some more.

At last he clutched his jacket collar around his neck and trotted through the drizzle to the back of the house. Maybe she was in the kitchen and somehow hadn't heard his knock. He dashed up the steps and opened the screen door of the back porch. "Anna?" he called, and walked across the porch to the back door.

She wasn't in the kitchen. He could see that from the window as he passed. For the first time, he acknowledged the corkscrew of fear in his gut. Something was wrong.

He tried the back door, and it opened. "Anna?" he called again, louder this time. No answer. If she was soaking in a bubble bath and really hadn't heard him, he'd apologize for walking into her house like this, but she was scaring him to death.

He covered the downstairs in no time and discovered the porch chair in the parlor, the weaving in progress and the wineglass on the hearth. He continued to call her name as he mounted the stairs, heart pounding. Either she wasn't in the house, and that didn't make sense with the fire smoldering and the wine still sitting there, or she was unconscious somewhere upstairs. He leaped up the remaining stairs and ran toward the bathroom. Most accidents happened there.

In a few minutes he stood panting at the top of the

stairs. She wasn't anywhere. He'd checked everything, even closets, in case she'd passed out for some reason while she was putting something away. She was nowhere in this house, unless Mrs. McCormick had forgotten to tell him about some secret room.

Charging back down the steps, he ran through the parlor and out to his truck. He jerked the passenger door open and fumbled with the glove compartment door. Finally, armed with a strong-beamed flashlight, he started a tour of the outside of the house while he continued to call her name.

He'd reached the backyard and rounded the woodpile, still shouting. Nothing. He thought of the path and rejected the idea that she'd be traipsing down it in this rain. But where else could she be?

Finally, in desperation, he picked out the outcropping of granite with his flashlight beam and plunged into the woods. This was madness. She wouldn't take the path at night, would she? And for what reason? Yet having no other solution to her disappearance, he jogged along the sodden ground as fast as the terrain and darkness would allow.

By the time he reached the edge of the woods and started through the rows of Christmas trees, he was ready to alert the police. No more fooling around, he thought, his heavy breathing pouring clouds of fog into the air in front of him. He'd call in the professionals, tell them to bring tracking dogs, fingerprint experts, whatever it took to get her back. He was numb with cold and fear.

He started running the last distance when he noticed a weak light reflected off the white clapboard siding of his house. And a shadow. Someone was there. Thinking it could be the same maniac who had abducted Anna, he snapped off his light and crept forward.

The person moved toward the parlor window and peered in. The light from the window shone on the top of carrot-red hair. Anna! His knees grew weak with relief. But what in hell was she up to? He thought of sneaking up behind her, just to get revenge for the way she'd scared him, but he couldn't do it.

Instead, he called out to her. "Anything interesting going on inside? Anybody running around naked?"

She gave a startled squeal and spun in his direction. "What are you doing out there?" she called.

"I'll bet I have a better explanation for being out here than you have for being up there, peeping in my windows."

"I wasn't peeping! I was just..."

"Yes?"

"Well, I wondered if..."

"This should be very good." He reached the side of the house and stood in front of her, face to dripping face. "Okay," he said, more interested in her story than in getting out of the drizzle, "what gives?"

The rain had darkened her hair, and damp ringlets clung to her forehead. Her eyelashes stuck together with the moisture, and her brown eyes seemed deeper and more velvety than ever before. "I don't suppose you've read Nancy Drew," she said.

"Afraid not."

"The Hardy Boys?"

"Yes, I did read those. Ah, I get it, you were out of reading material and wanted to see what was on my bookshelves. Makes perfect sense."

"No. I, um, thought I'd try some adventure of my own, and it backfired," she continued. "But I still don't understand what you're doing wandering around in your backyard in the rain at night."

"I finished all The Hardy Boys mysteries, and it seemed like the only alternative."

"Sam, be serious!"

"If you want serious, you should have caught my act a few minutes ago, before I spotted you doing your Inspector Clouseau routine. When I couldn't find you at your house, and the car was there and the wine and the fire, I got serious real fast."

"You came to my house?"

"Yep."

"And then came over on the path?"

"Bingo."

"Oh, Sam." She started to giggle and clapped her hand over her mouth. "I'm sorry," she managed, and giggled some more. "I've worried you, but honestly, I didn't mean to."

"What *did* you mean to do?"

"I...wondered if you were home or not, and if you were alone. I was...curious, and I thought it would be fun to sneak along the path to your house, investigate and sneak back without you knowing." She glanced up at him and her lips twitched, betraying her controlled impulse to smile.

"You were *spying* on me?"

"Yeah." She dipped her head, but not before he heard her muffled laughter.

"Why?"

Her laughter escaped and surrounded them. "I'm sorry I scared you, but I had no idea you'd show up at my place."

"I guess not."

"And come to think of it, I had a great time, even with the rain. Nancy Drew would have been proud of me. I accomplished my mission and discovered that you weren't home, except I thought you were out with someone else."

He grinned back at her. "That's what you wanted to know?"

"Uh-huh." Her laughter subsided into soft chuckles. "I'm caught, aren't I?"

"Uh-huh." He clicked off the flashlight with his thumb. "And now you have to pay the price." He drew her into his arms and relished every soggy point of contact as she came to him willingly. His lips met hers. She tasted like rain and wine, and something more intoxicating than either. She tasted of yes.

He kissed her as the rain soaked his hair and trickled inside the collar of his jacket. The heated welcome of her mouth made everything else unimportant, until the tension in his body demanded more than fevered kisses. He couldn't undress her here. Much as he didn't want to, he had to give up her yielding lips if he expected to gain all of her.

He lifted his head but kept her tight against him. "Let's go in."

"But your truck's at my house," she murmured.

"We don't need the truck for what I have in mind."

She gazed up at him. "But my house is still unlocked, and I left the fire, and—"

"Damn, you're right. We'll have to go back."

"You never said why you drove over."

"To invite you to supper." He leaned down to nibble at her lips. "But really for this." His fingers itched to unzip her jacket, but the air was too cold. "Come on. We'll check your fireplace and lock up before we drive over here."

"Why drive back here? I could fix you supper at my place."

"Because." He decided not to give her more answer than that and let her figure it out. Or contradict him. Maybe she was more prepared for this eventuality than he gave her credit for, but he didn't think so. Her boyfriend had left months ago, and by her own admission, she'd dated nobody since. Precautions during lovemaking were probably up to him.

"All right," she said softly. "Your house."

"We'll have to walk single file. Want to lead or follow?"

She hesitated. "Lead," she said, "if you'll loan me your flashlight. It has a stronger beam than mine."

"It's all yours," he said, and smiled as he handed it to her.

"That sounded like a loaded remark."

"It was."

"Sam, I want this with you. I really do. But I'm scared, too. What if I don't—What if we aren't—"

"Hey." He brought her in close again to increase her sense of security, and perhaps, his. "What happened to the courageous woman who set out on an adventure tonight? You think I'm not scared? You think I'm not afraid that you won't like the way I do things?"

"I guess that's logical, for you to be worried, too."

"Darn right. But I'll risk it, and I'm not putting all my money on the first encounter, either. We may have to experiment before we get the right combination. Can you live with that?"

He felt her relax against him, and her sigh, which seemed to take her fears with it, was worth the extra drenching they received for standing there like idiots in the rain. "Pleasure, not pressure," he murmured. "Ready?"

"Yes."

He released her and stepped aside. She switched on the strong beam of his flashlight and started down the path. Raising his eyes to the dripping skies above him, Sam mumbled a quick thank you to the powers that be for this incredible gift that almost hadn't been his tonight.

"I should change into dry clothes when we get to my house," she said over her shoulder.

"Just bring them," he said, knowing he couldn't stand around twirling his thumbs downstairs while she stripped upstairs. The very thought would send him straight up there into her bedroom, and that wasn't the right place for this to happen.

When they emerged into the clearing of her backyard, he moved up beside her and circled her waist with one arm. "I'll take care of the fire and lock the back door while you round up some extra clothes."

"All right."

"By the way, the weaving project looks beautiful. My grandmother would have liked it, I think."

"I'd meant to finish it tonight," she said as they held hands and climbed the steps to the screened porch.

"We'll come back early tomorrow. I'll cook for you, pack, whatever, so you can work, until you have to leave. I want to be an addition, not a detraction, in your life, Anna."

As they entered the kitchen, she smiled at him and squeezed his hand before releasing it. "I don't have much doubt which you are, Sam. I'll be right back."

He watched her go and then closed his eyes as anticipation gripped him with hot hands. Sure, he was a little scared, as he'd admitted to her, but his fears were almost nonexistent compared to the driving need in his loins. Maybe, just maybe, he could awaken the same force in her. He believed she was capable of blinding passion, but he might have to work a little to coax it to the surface. He looked forward to the task.

In minutes they'd locked her house and he was helping her up onto the seat of his pickup. "I should have a truck in the city," she said, settling on the tweed seat cover. "Much safer than my little compact."

"Or you could leave the city," he suggested before closing the door. Might as well start putting his cards on the table, he thought as he rounded the cab and climbed behind the steering wheel. Then he realized with a jolt the hand he was playing. They could be lovers without her leaving the city for good, but if she became his wife... He glanced at her to gauge her reaction to his last comment.

"My work is there, Sam."

"Work you're growing tired of."

"Maybe, but—"

"Never mind." He started the engine. "I didn't mean to talk about that now, anyway." He put his arm over the back of the bench seat and looked behind him as he backed down her driveway. Once on the farm road, he circled her shoulders and drew her close to him. "Besides, talking has its limits," he added, gazing into her upturned face. "How about shifting into first gear for me?"

She smiled. "Gonna make me work, huh?"

"Only in the interests of pleasure," he said, and gave her a lingering kiss. "And safety. There isn't much traffic on this road, but sure as we sit here, someone will come along and rear end this truck."

"Right." Anna grasped the knob of the floor shift and pushed it into first gear.

The rain had stopped, so Sam didn't have to fool with the windshield wipers, and they weren't going far enough for the heater to do much good, either. "I'll bet you're freezing," he said, nestling her closer after she finished the shifting procedure and they were in third.

"My own fault," she said. "You're the one who should be complaining. If it hadn't been for my trek into the woods, you wouldn't be all wet."

"If it hadn't been for your trek into the woods, I wouldn't know that you care about me, so don't expect complaints about a few damp clothes and a little chill in the air. Having you here is worth it."

She glanced at his profile, illuminated by the glow from the dash. "I'm glad I'm here."

"Good."

What a crazy way for the evening to turn out, she thought as they covered the short distance to Garrison's Christmas Tree Farm. Not long ago she'd been standing in the rain, convinced that he'd taken another woman out for the evening. She'd told Sam the truth about having fun with her little adventure; she hadn't mentioned how the fun had disappeared once she'd discovered that his truck wasn't parked in its usual place in front of his house.

And then, miracle of miracles, he'd shown up in his own backyard, and she'd forgotten how silly her mission would look to him in her relief that he wasn't with someone else, after all. She reflected briefly how Eric would have reacted if she'd pulled a stunt like that. Consequently, she hadn't pulled any stunts in a long time. If the result of taking chances was being here, soaked but happy in the curve of Sam's arm, she'd have to take more chances in the future.

Sam parked the truck and they hurried inside. "Stay right here," he said, leaving her in the parlor beside the blackened hearth. "I'll get you some towels and some warm things to wrap up in before I start the fire."

In a moment he was back with a pile of towels in his hands and his grandmother's blue woven blanket slung over his shoulder. "You can climb out of that wet stuff and dry off while I bring in some wood," he said, offering her the towels. "Then I thought you might like to wrap up in this." He laid the blue blanket across the pile.

"Sam..."

"Humor me, Anna. From the first time you touched this blanket, I've had a fantasy of seeing you wrapped in it." He tipped her chin up and captured her gaze. "For the sake of adventure?"

"And here I thought you were a conservative accountant, a sedate tree farmer."

"No, you didn't. You never thought that, or you wouldn't be here."

A sensuous thrill ran through her as she imagined the soft wool blanket caressing her bare skin. "Go get the wood," she said.

With a look that would melt a hole in the polar ice cap, he turned and left. She quickly nudged off her shoes and removed her sodden yellow sweat suit and damp underwear. With a whisk of the topmost towel, she dried her chilled skin and reached for the blanket. She was curled in it on the sofa when he returned with an armload of wood.

He stopped in the doorway and swallowed heavily. "Fantasies are such pale things next to reality," he said.

"Finish your work," she murmured, meeting his gaze.

Without a word, he walked to the fireplace and dumped the wood into the bin beside it. Then, with a glance back at her, he stripped off his jacket and flung it over one of the ugly vinyl chairs before hunkering down in front of the hearth to build the fire.

"I'm becoming obsessed with you, Anna," he said quietly, his back still toward her as he arranged kindling and larger pieces of wood on the grate. "I can't remember a woman ever getting underneath my skin this way. After all my lectures to myself, I still drove to your house tonight, just to have contact with you— any contact."

"You sound almost angry with me."

"I don't mean to." He shoved crumpled newspaper under the grate and struck a match. "But this feeling of wanting you is overwhelming." The flames licked upward from the paper and enfolded the kindling. As it caught fire and sent tongues of flame toward the large logs, he stood and turned toward her. "No matter how I try to laugh and joke, I still ache for you. Sometimes I think it will drive me crazy."

She trembled with excitement as he approached. The glow from the fire behind him and the lamp beside the sofa were all that lighted the room. The only sound was the pop and hiss of the flames moving greedily over the dry wood. Something awaited her in this room, something that would change her life.

"Have you ever wanted someone that much?" he asked, standing before her and slowly removing his shirt.

Unable to speak, she shook her head.

"I hope someday you will." He kicked away his shoes and unfastened his jeans. "And if I have any luck at all, that person will be me." Before he pushed his jeans over his hips, he reached into the pocket and took out a cellophane package, which he tossed on the end table beside the couch.

Then he continued undressing without modesty or flirtation, as if removing his clothes were an insignificant chore that he must perform. His full attention, reflected in the intensity of his gaze, was focused completely on her and the moment when he could take her in his arms.

His urgency, coupled with the sight of his aroused body, so hard and angular compared to hers, created a basic longing to mate with this man, this other, a longing that caught her by surprise. In place of sweet stirrings she'd experienced before, in place of pleasant, civilized desire, she knew the beginnings of raw hunger. Was this what he felt?

She expected him to lie with her on the sofa, for that to be their cushioned bower, but instead he swept her up in his arms and carried her to the braided rug before the fire. It was right, she realized as he settled her against the firm support of floor and braided cloth and lay beside her. There was nothing soft about this emotion between them, at least not this time.

"Anna." His voice was rough as he drew aside the blanket that covered her. His gaze followed the path of his caress over her breasts and her ribs. When his fingers tunneled through the curls below her flat stomach and found her drenched with wanting him, his breath caught and he closed his eyes.

"That," he whispered, gazing into her face as he stroked the aching bud of her desire, "is the nicest thing you can do for a man."

She clutched the back of his neck and moaned. "I'm beginning to understand...what you meant...about wanting," she said.

"That's good." Changing his rhythm but not the location of his hand, he leaned down to suckle her breast.

She arched like a hunter's bow drawn tight by the curl of his tongue and the coaxing flutter of his fingers. But when she thought she would snap, he seemed to know, and he paused to kiss his way to her other breast and run his knuckles lightly along the inside of her thighs.

Before long the assault began once more, and she tossed her head from side to side and cried out his name. "Is this what you meant?" she gasped. "The feeling is so... I can't...explain...."

He gazed up at her. "Yes, I know."

"Sam." She held his face, knowing she was begging. "Get whatever you threw on the table. Get it now before you drive me insane with this teasing."

"I like you when you're insane," he replied, but he rose and retrieved the package anyway. "You're sure you're ready for this to be over?" he asked gently, "because once I'm inside you, I can't promise forever."

"I haven't got forever," she replied, breathing hard. "Love me, Sam." And he did as she asked. When he pushed into her, she felt as if the cavalry had arrived, and she gladly met the charge. They'd both been right. Neither of them had forever. Neither of them had much time at all before the rush of completion overtook them and left them crying out with the depth of their satisfaction.

The impact left Anna limp and dazed but filled with overwhelming happiness. If she'd thought she knew what making love meant, Sam had just pointed out a huge gap in her education, a gap he seemed most willing to correct.

His torso slumped against her, and his head rested in the hollow of her shoulder. Judging by the brace of his elbows, she suspected he wasn't giving her his full weight, though. No matter how much passion drove him, he was the kind of man who wouldn't allow his lovemaking to be clumsy or selfish.

She traced her name across his back, and he lifted his head.

"Again," he murmured.

She wrote her name once more, made a plus sign under it, then wrote his name below that.

He smiled down at her. "You can say that again. Are you comfortable enough?"

"I feel terrific, but—"

"Yeah, this rug wasn't meant for long-term occupancy. I have an idea. I'll bring the mattress down from upstairs, and we'll stay here by the fire all night. How's that?"

"Lovely. Want some help?"

"That's okay. I'll do it," he said, easing away from her. "While I'm bringing down the mattress, you can stoke up the fire."

She glanced at him and lifted an eyebrow.

"Right. Both fires," he said, chuckling. "I'll also bring down more of those little plastic packages."

In short order the wood was crackling again in the fireplace, and Sam had created a cozy love nest for them in front of it.

"There," he said, stretching out beside her and pulling the blue wool blanket over them. "And if you're hungry, we can have a picnic right here."

Anna wrapped her arms around him. "I'm already having a picnic."

"So am I," he said, kissing her lightly. "Mmm." He returned for another sip. "So am I."

"I'd like to stay right here all weekend," she murmured between kisses.

"You won't get your weaving done that way."

"At this moment, I don't care."

Sam groaned softly and buried his face in the curve of her shoulder. "This isn't fair. I know the weaving is important to you—shoot, it may even be important to me. But so is making love to you, and you're only in Sumersbury forty-eight hours out of every week." He glanced up at her. "Think you could clone yourself?"

Anna chuckled. "This is kind of funny. All summer I sat around doing virtually nothing each weekend, and suddenly I'm sliding off in more directions than a centipede on roller skates."

"Just so you keep skatin' toward me, darlin'." Sam nuzzled her earlobe.

She enjoyed his use of an endearment, even if it was in fun. "I can't seem to help myself."

Sam lay quietly for a moment while Anna stroked his back. Finally he lifted his head and grinned at her. "I have the solution."

She tensed, certain he was about to ask her to quit her job and move in with him so that she'd have more than enough time for decorating his house, weaving and making love. The next step would be marriage. She wasn't nearly ready to make such life-altering decisions, but apparently he was.

"What's wrong?" he asked, his grin fading. "You look frightened to death."

"Sam, don't bring that up. Not yet, please."

9

"DON'T BRING WHAT UP?" Sam asked, frowning. "What could you possibly think that I—Oh, I get it." His puzzled expression changed to one of disappointment, and he glanced away. "Scared you, did I? That's certainly flattering."

"Sam, it's just that I..."

"It's not often a guy gets an answer to a question without asking it. At least I know where I stand, so I won't make any foolish assumptions."

Her heart wrenched at the knowledge that she'd hurt him. And unnecessarily, it seemed. He hadn't been thinking about living together or marriage at all. "I'm sorry," she murmured.

He looked into her eyes without saying anything.

"Sam, what are you thinking?" she asked, in agony over the damage she'd caused to their wonderful mood.

"If I told you, you'd only get scared again. You want to make love with no strings attached, right? Don't be afraid to tell me the truth, Anna. I just need to know the rules, that's all."

She swallowed the lump in her throat. "No rules,"

she said, laying her palm against his cheek. "Honest."

He took her hand and brought it to his lips. "I beg to differ. A minute ago you told me not to bring up a certain subject. That sounds like a rule to me. Are there any others?"

She dropped her hand and turned away. "I'm not ready to—"

"I get that, loud and clear. But what else? For example, a small example, am I allowed to say I'm falling in love with you?"

Heat flew to her cheeks, and a rushing sound filled her ears. Slowly she lifted her gaze to his. "Are you?"

"There's a distinct possibility."

Joy flooded through her, surprising her with its intensity. "Oh, Sam."

He stared at her in wonder. "You're happy," he whispered.

She nodded as tears pricked her eyes.

"You crazy woman." He slid his hand behind her hair and caressed her nape. Then he leaned over and kissed the outer corners of her eyes, where moisture gathered. "Haven't you heard the song about love and marriage going together like a horse and carriage?"

Anna's smile trembled. "For right now, could I just have the horse?"

His gaze was tender as he returned her smile. "I don't see why not."

She knew the moment was hers forever, no matter

what happened after it. Emotion nearly closed her throat, and she had to swallow twice before she could speak. "Am I allowed to say I'm falling in love with you?" she asked, gazing up at him.

The look in his eyes made her tears start afresh. "No rules with me," he whispered, as if he, too, had difficulty speaking. "None."

"Because I think I am. You've filled my life with more happiness than you'll ever know."

"Silly me," he said, his voice cracking. "Worrying about a dumb carriage." He kissed her wet cheeks, her nose and her eyelids. Finally, with a sigh, he fit his mouth to hers and pulled her soft, silky body close as the magic began once more.

LATE THE NEXT MORNING, they sat cross-legged on the mattress drinking coffee and discussing Anna's plans for the two remaining upstairs bedrooms, the dining room and the kitchen.

"Can we finish all that by the first week in December?" Sam asked.

She wrapped both hands around her coffee mug and savored his tousled, carefree appearance. They'd showered together, and he'd convinced her that getting dressed was useless until she was ready to leave for New York and they'd finally run out of time to make love. Consequently he'd put on his bathrobe and handed her one of his flannel shirts. "We can't finish the decorating if we spend all our time in bed," she teased, "if that's your question."

He stuck out his lower lip in a mock pout. "I was afraid you'd say that. Somebody sure messed up when they invented five-day weeks and two-day weekends. It should be the other way around."

"Speaking of that, what was your suggestion about my weaving? You never said."

He grinned. "I'm no fool. If a woman tells me she's falling for me and proceeds to show me in many delicious ways, I'm not about to change the subject."

Sensuous pleasure ran down her spine. "You'd better tell me your idea about the weaving," she said, putting her mug on the hearth and moving closer to him, "because I can feel that same distraction taking hold of me again."

"Oh, sweetheart, so can I." He leaned over and set his coffee on the floor. Then he pulled her onto his lap. "You have too many buttons fastened on that shirt."

"The weaving," she reminded him as he undid the buttons with practiced dexterity.

"Mmm." He slipped his hand beneath the shirt and cupped her breast.

"Sam, you're not listening." She marveled at how quickly she reacted to the lazy brush of his thumb across her nipple. All he had to do was look at her the way he was looking at her now and touch her like this, and she trembled with longing. "The weaving," she prompted without much conviction. "Tell me."

"It's simple," he murmured, continuing his caress. "We'll move the loom to New York."

"To New York?" Her concentration wasn't great, anyway, and she couldn't quite take in what he'd said.

"Sure. I'll follow you home in the truck." He ran the tip of his tongue around the curve of her ear. "Maybe you'd even invite me to spend the night."

"Sam," she protested weakly as he nibbled on her earlobe, "I can't have the loom. We're using it as a focal point in the parlor."

"I thought of that," he said, his breath warm in her ear. "Tessie has a loom, almost the same kind. We'll ask to borrow hers for a couple of days."

"But your grandmother's loom shouldn't be moved that far," Anna continued, unconvinced. "Something might happen to it."

"Nothing will happen." He eased her back onto the mattress and pushed the shirt away. "At least, not to the loom. I can't promise nothing will happen to you," he continued, kissing his way along her collarbone and moving down to the swell of her breast, "especially if you invite me to share your bed tonight."

"Oh." She sighed as he drew her nipple into his mouth.

He lavished attention on that part of her before finally lifting his head to gaze into her face. "Is that a yes?"

She reached for the belt of his robe. "With you, it seems to be the only word I know."

"And all you need to know," he said, tossing his bathrobe aside.

They made love slowly, each staving off their release as long as possible. After they finally succumbed to the pressure they'd built, they lay for a long time stroking and petting each other, postponing the moment when they'd have to leave the sensuous nest of their first lovemaking.

Eventually they could stall no longer. They dressed, ate a quick lunch and called Tessie about her loom. She agreed immediately to loan it for the TV special. Later, as Sam and Anna tied his grandmother's loom in the back of his truck, Anna continued to battle her fears. Although Sam's suggestion made sense, she couldn't shake her belief that Hilary Schute's loom didn't belong in New York City. During their drive in tandem down the turnpike, she kept looking in her rearview mirror, expecting some highway disaster to befall the loom.

When the New York skyline appeared, Anna tried to remember how she'd left the apartment. Fairly well picked up, she thought, and she'd put clean sheets on the bed because it had become her habit to do that before taking off on Friday. Coming home to fresh linens gave her a small reward for having to leave Sumersbury, although tonight she'd have more reward than that. She'd brought the most important attraction Sumersbury had to offer home with her, and she wasn't thinking of the loom, either.

She'd protested again about the inconvenience for

Sam, driving all the way to New York and all the way back home the next day. He'd insisted that on the way home Monday he'd stop off to take care of business with two clients, one in New Haven and one in Hartford. She suspected him of exaggerating the importance of those business calls, but in the end, she wanted him in New York tonight as much as he wanted to be there.

They parked in the underground garage beneath her apartment building and managed, with some maneuvering, to get the loom into the elevator. On the way up to the fourth floor, they smiled at each other across the wooden structure.

"This was a great idea," Sam commented. "Admit it."

"Once the loom's in my apartment and no harm has come to it, I'll admit it. Although that's not even considering the return trip." She glanced at him as she realized they'd never discussed the length of this loan. Two months? Six months? The length of their relationship?

"You've got that worried look again, Anna."

"We've left this deal—my design services in exchange for use of the loom—kind of open-ended. Are you aware of that?"

"Completely aware."

She gazed at him as the elevator bumped to a stop on the fourth floor. "I guess you're not too worried about getting your loom back."

"Oh, I intend to get it back." He leaned down to pick up his end. "Ready?"

"I think so," she said, although as she helped him carry the loom and directed him toward her door, she wondered how ready she was for Sam Garrison. When he retrieved his loom, did he expect that she'd be part of the bargain? Originally she'd viewed the loom as a symbol of growth in her life, a challenging new activity to expand her horizons. Was there a chance, a very small chance, that Sam viewed the loom as bait for a trap?

WHEN ANNA'S CLOCK RADIO clicked on the next morning with a traffic report, she reached for the Off button and realized she couldn't move—a man's arm held her firmly to the mattress. Sam was in her bed.

Sam, who had admired her framed print of children in the country, who had joked about the fact she'd replaced the futon with a real bed. Privately she'd decided that she'd replaced Eric with a real man. Now that she knew the fun of having Sam with her in New York, she'd miss him all the more when he left for Sumersbury today.

She turned her head on the pillow to gaze at him. His slow smile in the semidarkness recharged her like a first cup of coffee. The night before, in his arms, she'd put aside her misgivings about their future, and the glow from their loving still warmed her this morning.

"Hi," he said. "Sleep well?"

"You're the guest. I'm supposed to ask you that."

"The sirens woke me a few times, but it was worth it each time to be reminded I was in bed with you."

"What sirens?" she asked. "Were they close? I didn't hear anything."

"That's because you're a city girl, and they don't bother you anymore."

"Oh." She listened to the traffic report mention an accident on the Brooklyn Bridge before the station switched to music. In the street outside the apartment, the rush of cars and trucks was punctuated by honking horns. "I'll bet you don't wake up to an alarm each morning, either," she said. "Or impatient taxi drivers."

"No, I wake up with the sun."

"The buildings block it here. If I got up with the sun, I wouldn't be at work until noon."

He reached for her. "Let's pretend we're back in the country, then. Noon sounds about right to me."

"Sam, don't," she said, resisting him for the first time since they'd made love Saturday night. "I'll be late."

He rolled her onto her back and bent his face to her breasts. "But Sam has to go home today," he murmured, kissing her softness. "Sam won't be able to do this again until Friday."

"I know, but—please..." She tried to squirm away from him, but he held her fast with both arms and one strong leg. Slowly he licked and nibbled his way from one breast to the other. "I don't have time." She moaned, but her nipples grew firm and thrust toward him, nevertheless.

"Sure you have time," he murmured, and took the offering into his mouth.

"Then...hurry," she said, breathing hard. She'd already allowed this to go too far, and her body demanded satisfaction. She would be late to work, but maybe not very late.

Yet he wasn't going to hurry, she realized as the moist warmth of his tongue began a slow descent between her ribs to her navel. He was opening a new chapter in their book of loving. He'd released her hands and was touching her breasts as his kiss moved over her stomach. "Sam," she breathed, holding his head, stopping him from going lower. "Not now, Sam."

"Is that a rule?" he asked softly, lacing his fingers through hers and continuing to kiss her. "I can't do this on Monday mornings?"

"Not when I have to work," she protested, but her voice didn't convince even her.

"Tell me you'd rather be on time than have me do this," he said, kissing her inner thigh.

"You don't play fair," she gasped.

"Or this."

She writhed beneath the intensity of his caress. She became kindling, he the flame. There was no escape, but she no longer wanted one. She gave herself up to a shuddering, drenching climax. The room spun, and vaguely she knew that he'd sheathed himself and was hovering over her once more.

"The falling part is over," he breathed, and lifted her quivering hips. "I'm in love with you, Anna."

When he pushed into her, her body arched and the quickening began again. Incredibly, her body wanted more. She tightened around him and gazed into his face. "I love you, too," she whispered.

"You're going to be very late."

"I don't care."

His lips came down on hers in a crushing kiss. Then he braced his arms on either side of her head and loved her with a fierce rhythm that wrung cries of passion from deep in her throat. He held back, refusing to join her, and brought her to the heights a third time before the dam broke in him, as well.

It took her a long time to recover, to even have the strength to lift her hand and touch his back, slippery with sweat. She was shaken by the depth of passion she'd discovered. Or more accurately, that Sam had discovered. "I...I should get up," she murmured.

"I know," he said, his breath warm on her ear. "But I wish you didn't have to. I wish you didn't ever have to."

"Right now, so do I. That...was incredible. I had no idea that I could..."

"Neither did I," he admitted. "Glad you didn't leap out of bed this morning?"

"Yes. I'll have some creative explaining to do at the store, but yes."

"Don't worry about the people at the store. They can't hurt you."

"They can fire me, Sam."

"Would that be so terrible?"

She didn't answer him, because she didn't know the answer.

"I wouldn't let you starve, Anna. I love you."

Ah, how he tempted her! The job had become tedious, although lately her interest had picked up a little. But her New York existence seemed flat compared to what Sam offered—the country setting she craved, unlimited time to weave and loving as she'd never known.

"I love you, too, but you have to give me time to think," she said.

"If you're like my grandmother, you'll think while you weave."

"Yes." She knew then that he'd intended the loom to be at the very least his advocate while he was away from her. "Sam, I've always paid my way, and I couldn't make a living in Sumersbury."

He rolled onto his side and propped his head on his hand. "You don't know that yet. Make the decision to move to the country first, and then we'll talk about how you'll support yourself."

"I'd rather do it the other way around."

"Maybe, but I think your heart is making some decisions for you, and not in that order."

She smiled at him. "My heart isn't to be trusted, especially after the sort of thing that just happened to us."

"Oh, yes it is, Anna." He tenderly placed his hand over her left breast. "It most certainly is."

ANNA COMPLETELY MISSED the design staff meeting. She gave as her excuse that she'd been tied up in an early-morning appointment with a client, which was technically true, she reasoned. Over Sam's protest, she'd left the apartment without breakfast, and by noon she was ready to eat half the items on the menu of the store's lunchroom. She'd just ordered a Reuben sandwich when Vivian walked in and scanned the tables.

Spotting Anna, Vivian hurried over and sat down. "I was hoping you'd be here. Store gossip has it that you missed the design staff meeting, which you never do, and that you've been acting strange the rest of the morning. What gives?"

Anna sighed and leaned back in her chair. "It could take me all lunch hour to tell you about this. Maybe you'd better order something."

"Honey, I'll even buy your lunch if you'll fill me in. I'm dying of curiosity. According to Jimmy, his friend Ted thinks you're terrific, but you brushed him off. So I figure this guy from Sumersbury is in the picture, somewhere. Am I right?"

"You're right." Anna motioned to the waitress. "But whatever I tell you has to be in confidence."

"Wow. This gets better every minute." Vivian

glanced up at the waitress and ordered a chef's salad. "Was this man the reason you were late this morning?" she asked when the waitress left.

Anna nodded and warmth rose in her at the memory of exactly why she'd been late. She pushed the memory away, and starting with the encounter with Estelle in the Sumersbury grocery, she told Vivian the story of falling in love with Sam Garrison. Their lunch arrived in the middle of the tale, and by the time Anna finished talking, they'd eaten most of it.

"Amazing," Vivian said, spearing a quarter of a hard-boiled egg. "Old Ted never had a prayer, did he?"

"I guess not. I shouldn't have asked you to set that up for me, but there was an outside chance that I'd suddenly turned man-crazy. I needed to know."

"And instead you're crazy about one man."

"Yes."

"So, are you going to quit your job and move to Sumersbury?"

"Vivian, there's no work for me in Sumersbury."

"I think Sam could find plenty for you to do," Vivian said with a wink.

"I don't believe in living on a man's income. You know that."

"Well, then, don't. Market your weaving. You said yourself that his grandmother could have made money at it."

"Yes, but I don't know how much." Anna pushed her plate away and rested both elbows on the table.

"And I'll tell you something else, something I've hardly admitted to myself. I love the country, but I'm only in Sumersbury two days a week. What if I moved there and and discovered that it was a little too quiet and peaceful?"

"Only you can answer that, sweetie. But this Sam Garrison sounds like the sort who would keep you stirred up."

"Mmm." Anna hid her smile behind her clasped hands.

"Hey, gal, you have the look of a satisfied woman on your face. City or country, that counts for a lot."

"I know. Lord, don't I know. But I don't have a realistic picture of Sam's and my relationship, either, because on the weekends, when I've been with him, he hasn't been working, either with his trees or his clients' accounts. We've had an artificial situation where he could give me all of his attention."

"Well, old Auntie Vivian has a suggestion."

Anna laughed. "As always. I should have come running to you, instead of making you search me out in this lunchroom."

"Perhaps you don't quite appreciate me yet."

"I'll try harder," Anna said, chuckling. "What's your brilliant suggestion?"

"Spend a week of your vacation in Sumersbury, maybe the week before this Christmas tree extravaganza. Test your tolerance for small-town living before you commit yourself one way or the other."

"Vivian, that's inspired!"

"I know," her friend said with feigned modesty. "I do, however, charge a fee for this kind of insightful advice."

"Whatever you say. I'm so impressed with your idea that I'd grant you anything."

"Better hear it first. I swear, Anna, I've never known you to be this impulsive. Sam must be a powerful influence on you."

"He is," Anna acknowledged, "but I'm changing, too. I'm learning to take chances, to let loose. I think that started when I bought the house in Sumersbury. Every day I feel more adventurous, more free." She recalled again how wildly free she had become in Sam's embrace this morning. Was that a result of her changing image of herself? "Anyway," she said, "what's this favor?"

"I want you to invite Jimmy and me to Sumersbury during the filming of the television special."

Anna laughed. "You're kidding. It'll be a circus."

"I know!" Vivian clapped her hands. "That's why I want to be there. First of all, I've never seen anyone cut down a twenty-five-foot tree, let alone *the* tree that will stand in the White House. Second, I'm really curious about your little town and your new beau, and third, I'd love to sneak in front of the cameras so I could be on TV."

"You and everyone else," Anna said, chuckling. "They won't be able to see the tree for the forest of people, if you'll pardon the expression."

"Go ahead, make fun. I know you don't have the

lust for fame that grips most people. You just have to put us up for one night. I know you haven't invited anyone to your little farmhouse yet, but I thought that was because you were hibernating there, trying to forget Eric."

"I was."

"So I'm right again. Gosh, I'm good. But the hibernation is over, so can we come up?"

"Sure, why not? What kind of bed would you like?"

Vivian's eyes widened. "You have that many choices?"

"I have a whole catalog of choices. I don't have any bed in the house except mine, so I'll order you one. What do you want?"

"Now I feel guilty. We'll bring sleeping bags or something, Anna."

"Nonsense. I've had a growing urge to start decorating that house, anyway. Don't worry. I'll find a good buy, something on sale. It'll be fun."

"You're sure?"

Anna nodded. Yes, she wanted to fix up her house and the apartment, as well. Partly through Sam's influence and partly from her own new sense of self, she longed to give her surroundings the stamp of her personality.

10

THE FOLLOWING FRIDAY night Anna helped Sam drape the hallway and parlor of his house in preparation for stenciling the walls the next morning. With the sofa at the upholstery shop, the two vinyl chairs gone and paint cloths over everything, Sam's house looked cold and unromantic. Anna suggested they spend the night at her house, instead.

She talked Sam into bringing his harmonica, and after serenading her by the fire, he took her upstairs for a night of love. Charmed all over again by the warmth and simplicity of the country and her sweet country man, Anna began to believe in a life within the boundaries of Sumersbury.

They'd scheduled the next day full of activities—painting in the morning and quilt shopping in the afternoon—but Saturday night was reserved for a special treat. The sleigh bed would be finished on Saturday afternoon, and Sam insisted that he and Anna should take it for a test drive.

He thought it would be nice, too, if they could lie under a homemade quilt, although he wasn't thrilled with the idea of going through Estelle Terwiliger to find the right quilt.

"Now tell me again how Estelle wants to do this?" Sam asked as he moved his stepladder to the next section of undecorated wall in the parlor.

"She's asking all the women of the guild who have quilts to sell to bring them to her house and leave them there. Then we'll go over this afternoon, and if we like one, we can buy it from Estelle and she'll reimburse the woman who made it." Anna dipped her brush in forest green and filled in the stencil outline of a fir bough taped to the wall. At her request, Sam had borrowed a second stepladder so that they could work simultaneously.

"I suppose Estelle's plan is efficient," Sam grumbled.

"I think so."

"But I've had about enough of her."

"I know." Anna climbed down and repositioned her ladder. "Had about enough of stenciling, too?"

"Yeah, but we're almost done." He was impressed with her stamina, considering how little she was used to physical labor. She hadn't complained once, although she had to be getting tired. "I'm glad you decided the hall and the parlor were the only places we'd do this," he said, more for her sake than his. Christmas tree farming had toughened him up considerably, but Anna didn't have that advantage.

"I guess those two areas are enough," she said. "But if I had the leisure and could do it gradually, I'd have fun stenciling other rooms. Pineapples in the kitchen, for example. That's a traditional pattern, and

I can see a bright yellow border of them really adding a lot in there."

"You can stencil my walls anytime," Sam remarked, smiling. "Even after the TV cameras leave."

"Well, I just might," she said, acknowledging his flirtation with a glance. "But even without pineapples in the kitchen, the house will look great by December. I'm excited about the final product. I haven't enjoyed the design process this much in a long time."

"Good," he said absently, but as he continued working, he thought about her statement and frowned. Someone with career burnout usually didn't make comments like that. Once he'd switched to Christmas tree farming, accounting had become a necessary chore. He harbored a selfish hope that her enthusiasm for this project had to do with him instead of the work itself. From what he could tell, she was still bored with her New York assignments.

Still, he recalled that she'd sounded happy about the dresser scarf she'd woven and incorporated into a client's bedroom design. The woman wanted more of Anna's work in her home, and Anna had talked about presenting her woven designs to other clients, as well. He'd chosen to interpret the trend as a sign that Anna was moving toward a career in weaving and away from interior design. He had to agree with her that interior design wouldn't sustain her in Sumersbury. But weaving was a different story.

Anna seemed so contented when she was in Sumersbury that it had to be the right environment for her. She'd resisted giving up the proven income of interior design, and he understood that. Her weaving might never bring in as much money as her present career, but if she married him and lived a simple country existence, her paycheck wouldn't matter. She needed to get used to the idea, he concluded. Change took time.

"When we finish, I'll be ready for lunch," he said, moving his ladder again. "I thought you might enjoy a picnic in a secret place."

She laughed. "Now, Sam, I promised Estelle we'd be there by two, and it's nearly noon. We have to save our hanky-panky for the sleigh bed."

"Woman, how you misjudge me!" he said, pretending to be insulted. "Do you think every time I say the word 'picnic' I mean 'seduction'?"

"Yes."

"Well, you're right, but this time I promise to restrict myself to a few soul-shattering kisses."

"Okay," Anna said, chuckling. "What is this place, a childhood hideaway?"

"Nope, but it sure is secret. Classified, even. Can I trust you?"

"Implicitly, Agent Garrison. What have you got around here, a missile site?"

"A Christmas tree site. Only me, my foreman, John, and two White House aides know where the tree is. Want to be part of that elite group?"

Anna raised her eyebrows. "I don't know. Do I?

What if enemy spies take me hostage and shoot me full of truth serum?"

"I'm willing to take the chance. Besides, I need your advice about a spot for the pond that Estelle wants. John's no good at spatial relationships."

"I had no idea the tree's location would be so hush-hush," Anna said, attacking the last section of stenciling for her half of the room. "Why would anyone care where the tree is growing?"

"The White House aides explained that some nut might decide to make a political statement by vandalizing the tree or something. I think that's unlikely, but I have to play by the rules."

"Would you like to blindfold me and lead me there?"

"Anna, my love, I would trust you with my life, so I think I can trust you with a Christmas tree.... There, I'm done with that strip," he said, climbing down from his ladder.

"And I have only a little to go on this wall."

"While you finish that, I'll make the sandwiches," Sam volunteered.

Half an hour later they bumped along the dirt road that led from behind Sam's house and up a gentle slope dotted with elms and maples in full autumn color. Then the terrain leveled out into a meadow, and Sam stopped the truck. Farther up the road, where the hill became steep again, stood a phalanx of evergreens. Wide lanes separated each line of trees. Unlike the baby firs and spruces Anna had seen in front and to the side of Sam's house, these were well over six feet tall, with even taller trees in the rows behind them.

"There's a small stream running through this meadow," Sam explained, pointing. "Right now it's pretty overgrown with grass and weeds, but I could dam it up and make a pond for Estelle. The TV van would have to go right by it, so if she wants her skaters to be on display, they'd be right on the way to the cutting site. What do you think?"

"It would be beautiful, especially covered with snow," Anna said. "If you're willing to take the trouble, I'm sure Estelle would be overjoyed."

"The darn thing might not freeze," Sam added.

"That you can't control. I also assume you have liability insurance in case a skater falls."

Sam groaned. "I have all the insurance I need, but Lord, what a mess this could be."

"You could also tell Estelle you won't do it," Anna suggested.

"She's already got some teenagers excited about being on TV. I know all of them, and three of the boys help me cut and stack trees during the sales season. I can't disappoint those kids."

"You're a real softy, you know?"

"I know. Besides that, the TV people called this week, and I mentioned Estelle and her plans. They asked if she was the mayor, and when I said that the mayor takes orders from her, they wanted her name and number. They plan to coordinate directly with her. They sounded delighted with her ideas and said that a network senior executive had been afraid the special would be dull."

"Nobody should worry about that," Anna said, laughing. "Looks like you're really caught, Sam."

"Yep. Oh, well, by Christmas the circus will be over." He started the truck again and swore good-naturedly when it jolted over a pothole. "I'll have to grade this before December, too. I imagine Estelle would like me to pave it and put in curbs. That woman..."

"You've known her a long time, haven't you?"

"All my life. She's the one who advised my grand-father to plant Christmas trees on this unusable slope. In her typical bossy way, she found him a cut-rate price on seedlings and kind of forced him into trying it."

"No wonder she feels proprietary about the tele-vision special."

"That's right. Chances are the White House tree is one of those first seedlings that Estelle pushed on my grandfather thirty years ago. He bought some on his own soon after that, so I'm not really sure, but this honor belongs partly to Estelle."

"I'm glad you told me that," Anna said. "And when did you start helping your grandfather with the trees?"

"When I grew as high as the shovel. I can still re-member the first summer I helped plant."

"Wasn't it hard to dig here? I see a lot of rocks."

"There are a lot of rocks, believe me. That wall on the far side of the house is what we took out while we planted. Considering the slope and the rocks, Christmas trees is about the only crop this hillside could grow. I have to give Estelle credit."

Anna gazed at the wide rows of evergreens. "Is it hard to cut down trees your grandfather and you planted?"

"No, because I don't kill the tree. Whenever possible I use stump culture. See that?" He slowed down and pointed to a stump with a single sturdy limb growing from it. "Now look through the rows, and you'll see others. Cutting these trees is a little like shearing sheep. It works especially well with Fraser firs, which most of these are."

"How about the White House tree? Will you keep that stump?"

"Especially that one. To show my grandchildren."

Anna knew he meant it. Despite not being married yet, Sam fully expected to have children and grandchildren someday. Tradition and family were crucial to him.

"Not many of these have been cut," Anna said as they passed trees nearly twenty feet tall.

"No. Most are too big for Christmas trees, unless a city hall wants one, or the president of the United States." He stopped the truck. "Here we are."

"Where is it?"

Sam pointed to his left. "Down this row and five trees in."

"You don't have to worry about me giving away your secret," Anna said, peering past him at the giant trees. "One looks about like another to me, and I'd probably never find this particular row again."

He laughed. "I guess it's like being parents of twins. I wonder how anyone *can't* tell these trees apart." He opened his door. "Come on, let's go hobnob with greatness."

Sam carried the picnic basket, and Anna tucked an old blanket under one arm. Despite the blanket, Sam had assured her they'd have a sedate picnic. Anna glanced at her watch. Considering that it was now almost one o'clock, they didn't have time for anything but a sedate picnic.

"Here it is, all seven hundred pounds of it."

Anna stared upward at the immense fir tree. "I was wrong," she said. "I could find this one again. It's magnificent, Sam. I'm sorry you have to cut this beauty down."

"Me, too."

"Really? But you'll let another grow from the stump, right?"

"Sure, but I'll be sixty by the time it reaches the same height. Giants like this aren't quickly replaced."

Anna glanced at the freshly cut stump on the far side of the White House tree. "What happened to the one beside it?"

"That was the tree I entered in the contest, the twin, so to speak, of this one." He glanced at her. "I've been trained in business, and my business sense told me to take part in that contest. I won't again." He gazed down the row of firs. "I may never cut another of these big trees."

"I understand," Anna said softly.

"I've justified it this time because the White House tree will give joy to so many people, but I'm still not certain it's worth the sacrifice, and I don't want to keep justifying."

"But what about the other trees you cut, the smaller ones?"

He shrugged. "I'm not as sentimental about those, I guess because the tree can grow back in a few years. And some I sell as live trees, which is even better. They'll end up in somebody's front yard and eventually be this size."

"Your reasoning makes perfect sense to me."

He smiled at her. "I figured it would to someone who's careful not to step on cherished memories when she redecorates a house." He put down the picnic basket. "Let's eat."

Sam was as good as his word, and except for one lingering kiss before they climbed back into the truck, he didn't initiate any love play between them. They returned to his house with twenty minutes to spare before their appointment with Estelle Terwiliger.

"I'm glad you showed me the tree," Anna said as they drove to Estelle's house. "And I'm glad it's the last big one you plan to cut down."

"The town won't like that, so I don't plan to tell

anyone just yet. They'd as soon have me win the contest every year, I think."

"They'll have to come up with some other way to put Sumersbury on the map, that's all."

He smiled at her. "Yeah, like having a renowned weaver in town."

"Was that a gentle nudge or a strong push I just felt?"

He groaned and cursed himself inwardly. "Sorry."

"Apology accepted."

But their interchange dampened the mood, and they rode in silence the rest of the way to Estelle's house. She lived in a powder-blue Cape Cod a block from the main street of Sumersbury.

"Is there a Mr. Terwiliger?" Anna asked when they pulled onto the concrete driveway.

"Used to be. He died about five years ago. I could say that widowhood made Estelle a busybody, but it wouldn't be true. She's always minded everyone else's business."

"She's spreading rumors around town that we're lovers. Did you know that?"

Sam reached for her hand. "Yes, I knew that. Frankly, that's one rumor that makes me proud," he said, kissing her fingertips.

"We're about to choose a quilt for your bed," Anna pointed out, "the bed that we'll pick up today from the man who's refinishing it. I wonder if tonight I'll feel as if the whole town is at the keyhole, watching us."

Sam laughed. "You'll learn to ignore that feeling. And I promise to do everything in my power tonight to help you ignore it."

"Sounds nice."

"It will be." He opened his door. "Come on, let's buy a quilt to cuddle under. I think I'll specify to Estelle that we want a very *soft* quilt. That should keep the gossips in business."

"Sam!"

His blue eyes sparkled as he helped her down from the seat. "They only pry because they're jealous."

"And you're incredibly smug."

He slipped his arm around her waist and drew her close. "Yes, ma'am, I am."

Estelle's living room, overflowing with ceramic figurines, dishes of papier-mâché fruit and numerous dried flower arrangements, was made even busier by the quilts draped across two sofas and four chairs.

"My goodness," Anna exclaimed as Estelle ushered them through the foyer and into the room. Anna felt as if she'd stepped into a craft bazaar.

"Amazing, isn't it, what a little time and ingenuity can produce?" Estelle said. "All the accessories in this room are handmade, either by me or a member of our guild. By the way, I understand you're a weaver, Anna."

Shoot, Anna thought. *Here it comes, an invitation to join the guild.* "I'm only a beginner, Estelle."

"Now, now, don't be modest. The guild welcomes all levels of ability. We meet here on Wednesday evenings. I know that presently that isn't convenient for you, but perhaps someday it will be." She smiled conspiratorially at Sam.

"Perhaps," Anna mumbled, not looking at Sam.

"And Sammy," she said, laying her hand on his arm, "I'm glad to report the preparations for December are moving like clockwork. The television people are so accommodating. I've found a pair of antlers for the deer, and Tommy Andrews thinks he can rig up a blinking red nose. Can you imagine that?" Estelle glowed like an old-fashioned Christmas tree light.

"Not too easily," Sam admitted.

"We'll have quite a spectacular show, I can tell you. The choir and the orchestra are in rehearsal, and the shop decorations will be—But here I am running on and forgetting my manners. Let me take your coats. Can I get you something to drink, or perhaps some cookies? Homemade."

"Thanks, but we just had lunch," Anna said, removing her nylon jacket and handing it to Estelle.

"I'll bet Sammy could do with some cookies, couldn't you?" She beamed at him. "You never were one to turn down homemade cookies."

Sam grinned sheepishly. "Oatmeal-raisin?"

"That's right, your favorite. I'll bring in a plateful." She carried away the coats without waiting for further comment.

"You are putty in that woman's hands," Anna teased.

"To her I'll always be seven years old, I guess."

"Maybe that's because you act seven years old around her."

"I forgot that she makes those cookies until I walked in the door and smelled them. I have a weakness for Estelle's oatmeal-raisin cookies."

"So I see."

"You don't by any chance make—"

"Never," Anna said.

He shrugged. "Oh well, can't have it all."

"Here we are," Estelle announced, reappearing with a mounded plate of cookies and a napkin. She handed the whole thing to Sam. Enjoy yourself."

Anna coughed to keep from laughing at the delight on Sam's face as he picked up the first cookie and bit into it. Then he seemed to remember his manners and held out the plate to her. "Sure you won't have one?" he mumbled around the bits of cookie in his mouth.

"No, thanks, really. I'll start looking at these quilts, if you don't mind, Estelle."

"By all means." Estelle bustled in front of Anna and launched into a sales pitch for each of the quilts in turn, with Sam trailing behind.

Anna was grateful that the plate of cookies kept Sam's mouth full so he couldn't make his threatened remark about wanting a "very soft" quilt. Anna conducted her conversation with Estelle on an impersonal note while they discussed colors and patterns.

Aided by Sam's nods of approval, Anna narrowed the choice, eliminating all but two of the quilts. Both featured shades of blue, and either would complement the blue woven blanket Anna was using as the focal point of the bedroom. The prices were about the same.

She turned to ask Sam which he liked, but the merriment in his gaze worried her. She flashed him a warning look as he swallowed the last of the cookie he'd been eating.

"I've been listening to all this talk about color and design," he said, "but it seems to me nobody's brought up the most important quality to be considered."

Anna clenched her teeth.

"As the person who will be using this quilt, the thing I'm most interested in is—" he paused and winked at Anna "—sturdiness," he finished, gazing mildly at Estelle. "I'm a practical guy."

"Well, of course you are," Estelle said. "Most men are. So I'll tell you, in confidence, that the starburst pattern that Delores made is stitched more carefully, with better thread, than the garland-patterned quilt Jane made. If you ever repeat that to either of them, I'll deny saying it, but the fact is, Delores's quilt will wear like iron."

Anna let out her breath. "That settles it for me, then," she said. "I liked the starburst better, anyway. Sam, do you want to buy that one?"

He set the empty plate on an end table and wiped his hands on the napkin before walking over to the starburst quilt. He picked up a corner and fingered it gently. "Yes," he said, "this will do fine."

Anna knew he'd just made his softness test, but despite his teasing before they'd walked into the house, he'd had no intention of embarrassing her in front of Estelle. Anna felt her level of trust move up a notch.

"I'll get you a bag for it," Estelle said, picking up the empty plate. "More cookies, Sam?"

"Thanks, but I'm stuffed."

"I'll wrap up a few for you to take home, then." She left again without waiting for his reply.

"Sam, you finished off that whole plate!" Anna said when Estelle was gone.

"I needed something to do with my hands," he murmured. "Watching you wandering around looking at quilts while I imagined how you'd look under each of them, naked, had me in a state of—"

"Sam, for heaven's sake!" Anna glanced over her shoulder toward the hallway, where Estelle would reappear at any moment.

"We picked the right one, though," he continued, smiling at her. "That blue starburst will look terrific with your hair all spread out on the pillow, and your—"

"Will you stop? I—"

"She's coming down the hall," Sam muttered out of the corner of his mouth.

"I think these women do wonderful work," Anna said in a normal tone.

"Yes," Estelle agreed. "The quilts are very time-consuming. I don't have the patience for them, myself, so I admire those who do. Here's your bag of cookies, Sammy."

"Estelle," he protested, "you really shouldn't send me home with these."

"Nonsense, I enjoy baking."

Anna had a sudden inspiration. "How about gingerbread cookies? Do you make those during the holidays?"

"Why, yes, generally even a gingerbread house for my grandchildren, if they're coming here for Christmas."

"Estelle, would you consider baking some holiday shapes in gingerbread and selling them to me to use in decorating Sam's house? I could hang them in the windows, or maybe from the beams."

"I would consider baking them, but I'd never charge Sammy for cookies."

"But—"

"No charge," Estelle said, looking immovable, "or no deal. I'll even do a gingerbread house for you, if you like."

"I—that would be wonderful," Anna said, giving way before Estelle's approach just as Sam had earlier.

"After all," Estelle added, "Sammy needs *somebody* to bake for him."

Anna winced.

"Now you know, Anna," Estelle continued, "that if you need any other decorative items, things the guild can supply, you have only to ask. As you can see, we have many lovely things." She swept her arm around the room.

"I'll keep that in mind," Anna said, knowing that she had to be careful or Estelle would arrive with a truckload of crafts and insist on arranging them all over Sam's house. "For now, the quilt and the gingerbread will do nicely."

"Then let's get this folded up and in the bag for you," Estelle said, turning toward the sofa where the starburst quilt lay. "Anna, you can help me fold."

As Anna picked up the corners of the quilt, she thought about Estelle's implication that Sam was deprived because he had no woman to bake for him. The idea rankled. Worse, Anna suspected that Sam might agree with Estelle. Gradually, Anna was figuring out the job description for a rural wife, and domesticity was high on the list of attributes. Did Sam imagine that she was domestic?

He well might, she concluded as they took the quilt and said their goodbyes to Estelle. On their first evening together, Anna had fixed him a meal and indicated her interest in weaving. And what could be more home oriented, in his eyes, than interior design? She realized that if Sam viewed her as domestic, she also hadn't done much to correct the picture.

Late that afternoon, after they'd brought the refinished sleigh bed home and she was helping him put it together, Anna decided to set the record straight. "I really don't bake cookies, you know," she said, handing him a rubber mallet to tap in the dowels.

"I'm sure you don't, with your schedule." He attached the headboard to one side rail and picked up the footboard.

"No, I mean that I have no *desire* to bake cookies, even if I had all the time in the world."

He positioned the footboard and glanced up. "What's all this about baking cookies? Did I say I wanted you to bake cookies?"

"Not exactly, but you asked about it while we were at Estelle's," she said, bracing the footboard in place for him.

"Well, I was probably kidding you, whatever I said." Sam returned to his task. He fastened the footboard on both sides and moved to the last connection on the other side of the headboard. Finally he stepped out of the frame and reached for the slats that held the mattress and box spring. "Anyway, how do you know what you'd enjoy if you didn't have such a high-stress job?"

"I suppose I don't know that," Anna admitted, helping him fit slats across the width of the bed, "but I realized today that you may have a picture of me as a real homebody because of the weaving, and my career is sometimes seen as a feminine one, and—"

"Homebody." Sam turned and gazed at her as a slow grin spread across his face. "Now there's an interesting concept. Yeah, I think of you as a homebody. Every time I touch your body, it feels like home."

"Sam, that's not what I—"

"Give me a hand with this box spring, will you?" He seemed to be ignoring her explanation.

"Sure, but what I'm trying to say is that I'm not very domestic, despite the impression you might have of me." She helped him ease the box spring onto the frame, and together they slid the mattress in place.

"Let me tell you what impression I have of you," he said, walking around the bed. "Better yet," he added, grabbing her and tumbling with her onto the mattress, "let me demonstrate."

"We haven't even finished," she said, laughing as he began undressing her.

"Close enough," he said, unhooking her bra and tugging at her sweatpants and underwear. Within seconds he'd pulled both past her ankles and tossed them over the side of the sleigh bed. "Now, about impressions. I love this one." He massaged her breast with lazy circles of his palm. "When your nipple tightens, it makes a terrific impression on me," he murmured into her ear.

"Mmm..." Anna stretched her arms over her head and arched her back.

"Oh, my love..." He slid his arm beneath her and sipped at her uplifted breasts. "Talk about impressions," he whispered against her skin.

Anna's body heated as his gentle suction telegraphed passion down to the epicenter of her desire. Still clothed himself, he moved between her uncovered thighs and nudged the warm, moist spot there to encourage the tremors that would soon become an earthquake of sensation.

"You make a few...impressions of your own," she said unevenly.

"You like that impression?" He rubbed the wear-softened denim gently back and forth and gazed into her eyes.

"I do." Holding his gaze, she reached blindly for the buttons of his shirt. She fumbled with the task as he continued moving sensuously against her. "I want you so much."

He smiled. "That's the idea."

"Oh, Sam," she moaned, wrenching the last button out of its buttonhole. "Sam, I need—"

"Me, too." He levered himself away from her. "I think I'll take these off and impress the heck out of you," he said, breathing hard as he rolled away to strip off his jeans.

"Egotist."

"We'll see." Before long he hovered over her and teased her with small thrusts. "Impressed yet?"

"Not yet," she fibbed, gasping as he stoked the blaze within her.

"Yet?" He pushed a little farther.

"No."

"Sure takes...a lot...to impress you," he choked out. "Here goes." He buried himself in her with a groan.

"I'm...impressed," she whispered as he began a deep, penetrating rhythm. He brought her to the heights with long, sure strokes that coaxed murmurs and squeaks from the sleigh bed and cries of love from her.

"And I love you," he whispered, accelerating the pace. "More than anything...in the...world. Anna, now, Anna—yes!"

For a sweet, measureless time they swirled in the eddies of their own creation. Then gradually contentment settled around them, and they were still.

Moving with lazy delight, Sam propped himself on his elbows and smiled down at her. "I think we impressed each other that time."

"I agree." She returned his smile. "You give a whole new meaning to the idea of a sleigh ride."

Sam threw back his head and laughed. "That's right. This was supposed to be a significant event, trying out this bed."

"It was pretty significant to me."

"Yes, but did you think about the bed while we made love?"

"Can't say that I did. Only afterward."

"Me, either. So much for the importance of atmosphere. I guess it just proves that when I'm loving you, I can be happy on any flat, relatively soft surface," he said. "But the bed is nice," he added. "I think we'll go for lots of sleigh rides in the future."

"I'd like that."

"Me, too. I wish we weren't limited to weekends, though."

"That reminds me, Sam. What if I took some vacation time and spent the week before the tree cutting ceremony here?"

"In this bed? Fantastic!"

"In Sumersbury, crazy man."

"Darn. Well, having you in Sumersbury for a whole week is a start, and I'll work on the rest."

"You're a dreamer," she said, reaching up to kiss him lightly. "You'll be very busy that week."

"Not that busy. I love your idea. I haven't been looking forward to this whole shindig, but now I can hardly wait, if I can have you around for a week beforehand."

"Then I'll do it. I can finish all the last-minute Christmas decorations then, and...see how I like being here for longer than a weekend." She glanced at him nervously. Would he bristle at the idea of a test?

He didn't. "You'll love it," he said. "Homebody or not, you belong here, Anna."

"In this bed?" she teased, partly to avoid agreeing or disagreeing with him. She wasn't ready to do either yet.

"That, too," he replied, leaning down to capture her lips once again.

11

THE SATURDAY AFTER Thanksgiving, Anna took the Sumersbury exit off the turnpike and headed for her week in the country. She'd stuffed her car with supplies for Vivian and Jimmy's visit the following weekend and last-minute purchases for Sam's house: candles, lights, ribbons and ornaments. She'd found a good sale on poinsettias, and a dozen plants were propped in the back seat, along with rolls of rustic-looking wrapping paper to create make-believe packages under the tree.

She planned to unload her personal supplies at her house before going over to Sam's. He was too busy to spend any time with her this afternoon, anyway. Their peaceful weekends had been usurped by the Christmas tree season.

As she approached his farm, she heard chain saws buzzing, and a large truck with a tarp-covered load of trees rumbled out of his driveway as she passed. For the next three weeks, crews would work every day cutting trees to be shipped elsewhere. Local customers arrived to dig or cut their own trees between seven in the morning and nine at night.

Belatedly Sam had realized how little time he'd

have with Anna and had suggested she take a week during Christmas, instead. But Anna thought this week would be an excellent test of her endurance in the country. If she was to live here, she couldn't depend on Sam to keep her constantly entertained.

Besides, she needed to finish the holiday decorating of his house. He'd also suggested she include Thanksgiving and the Friday after as part of her vacation, but she couldn't spare time from her projects at work. As it was, she'd spent Saturday morning tying up loose ends and hadn't left the city until noon.

During the drive to Sumersbury, she'd waited for the lift of spirits that was supposed to accompany going on vacation. Instead she felt ambivalent. Spending each night with Sam would be wonderful, but as luck would have it, her work in the city was becoming more interesting every day, and she'd had to leave several projects hanging until her return. Weaving had added a new dimension to her career, and she relished introducing her own creations into decorating schemes.

She wasn't ready to sort out what her renewed interest in design meant. Perhaps after this week, she'd be choosing between two appealing alternatives: a career in weaving and residing in the country year-round; or a continuation of the way she was living now, with her time split between city and country.

Leaving her car in her driveway, she unlocked the house and carted her supplies inside. In the process she admired what she'd accomplished in the past few weeks. By watching sales, she'd found an excellent buy in a floral print sofa and a burgundy Queen Anne wing chair. Sam had unearthed a couple of end tables that had been stored in his barn and were in amazingly good shape, and she'd found a brass lamp that looked far richer than its price.

Upstairs she'd created a guest room for Vivian and Jimmy with a brass bedstead a client had wanted to sell and old barrels Sam had given her as nightstands. She'd used swags of decorative sheeting to soften the tall, narrow windows and covered the bed with an inexpensive hobnail spread and a generous array of accent pillows, including two that she'd woven the covers for herself.

Just putting one or two of her woven items in a room made the decor come alive for her. If she stayed in interior design, her weaving would be what kept her fresh for the task. She wondered if she ever would have rediscovered weaving without Sam. Someday, perhaps, but maybe not before she'd left interior design for another career.

After leaving her supplies in the kitchen, she locked the house and hurried through the cold to her car. The air smelled good, crisp with a hint of wood smoke, and the landscape reminded her of a hand-painted Oriental screen—soft beige hills, curving rock walls and dark tree branches leafless against a gray winter sky. Snow hadn't hit Connecticut yet this year, and all the residents of Sumersbury anxiously watched the weather report each night. Nature had only a week left to make a Currier and Ives print of the countryside for the television special.

Anna drove the short distance to Garrison's Christmas Tree Farm and parked in front of the house. Sam's truck was gone, but she'd expected that. She started carrying poinsettias into the house.

"Hi, Anna!" John called from over by the barn. He was supervising three boys as they wrapped heavy twine around trees to compress the branches and conserve moisture. A cache of trees was kept in the barn for local customers who didn't want to cut or dig their own. "Sam's out with a couple guys getting that pond filled," John shouted across the yard. "Said to tell you he'd be back soon as he could. Need any help with that?"

"Thanks, but I don't have much," Anna called back, and continued into the house with a poinsettia in each hand. She'd met John two weeks ago, when work at the farm picked up, and he'd had to put in some Saturday hours. They'd hit it off.

John looked more like a Christmas tree farmer than Sam, Anna thought. For one thing, he was older than Sam by at least twenty years, and his weathered face exuded experience. Everyone knew when John was around; he delivered both commands and jokes in a booming voice that resonated out of his barrel chest.

Anna finished carrying everything inside, hung her winter coat in the hall closet and breathed in appreciatively. At her instruction, Sam had set up undecorated trees in every room and a pile of boughs lay on a sheet of plastic by the door. Outside the evergreen scent was scattered by space and breezes, but inside the fragrance gathered in full force.

The aroma of gingerbread mingled with pine. Anna walked into the kitchen to find an elaborate frosted and candy-coated house on the counter and a shirt box beside it. Anna lifted the cover and discovered neat rows of gingerbread Santas, trees, stars and bells, all with ornament hangers baked into the tops. *She should be allowed to sing the whole score of the* Messiah *in exchange for this,* Anna thought, marveling at Estelle's careful workmanship.

The back door opened and she glanced up as Sam came in and gathered her up for a bear hug. "Merry Christmas," he said, pressing his cold cheek against hers. "I thought you'd never get here."

"Sam, this will be so much fun. Everything smells wonderful."

"Especially my decorator," he said, nuzzling the curve of her neck.

She shivered with delight at his caress and had the selfish wish that he could drop all his work and make love to her this very minute. She wasn't used to having Sam around without having him to herself. This week would be a lesson in patience. "How's the pond coming along?" she asked, trying to forestall the urges of her body.

"When I hold you like this, I don't give a damn," he replied. "Lord, you feel good. I love touching you." He slid both hands up her rib cage and cupped her breasts.

"I love it when you do." She locked her hands behind his neck and gazed up at him. "But I think your work crews will miss you if we indulge in what I'm thinking about."

"Yeah, you're right, doggone it. But tonight seems so far away."

"We'll stay busy," she said, kissing him lightly. "I have plenty to do in here, and I'm sure you have plenty to do out there."

"Unfortunately."

"Thanks for setting up the trees and bringing in the pine boughs. And Estelle's work is amazing, Sam. I hope you thanked her."

He grinned. "She'll have her reward. The television people promised to interview her as the town's 'holiday chairwoman' and lifelong resident of Sumersbury. I couldn't give Estelle a higher payment than national stardom, brief though it will be."

"You'll be a star, too, you know. Ever thought of that?"

"Not especially."

"Women from all over the country will see you in the middle of this romantic country setting and fall in love with you," Anna predicted, smiling. "Offers will come pouring in."

"There's only one offer I'm interested in," he said, combing his fingers through her riot of red hair.

"Only one woman I want to capture with this 'romantic country setting.'"

"I think she's already half in the bag."

"That's good. I—damn, I think John's calling me."

"I think so, too. You'd better go."

He kissed her quickly and opened the back door. "Be right there, John!" he called. Then he turned back to her. "Before I forget, Tessie's coming by with her loom this afternoon. She offered to help you if you needed her."

"I'd like that. I haven't seen her in a while."

"Will you decorate some of the trees today?"

"I'll probably get started. We have a lot to do, Sam."

"Save the big tree in the parlor, okay? I'd like to trim that one with you. We'll put some carols on the stereo tonight and get in the spirit."

"Aren't you sick of Christmas trees by now?"

"Believe it or not, no. I love this."

"Then it's settled," Anna said, enjoying his enthusiasm. "We'll decorate the tree tonight, together."

"And take a sleigh ride afterward," he said with a wink. "Bye, sweetheart."

"Bye." She watched him trot over to the barn and confer with John. What more could she want in life than to live with a man like Sam? In this fragrant, cozy house, held by his strong arms, the importance of her job in the city faded. Returning to the parlor, Anna hummed a tune while she unpacked candles and ribbons. She laughed when she realized the tune was "Sleigh Ride."

An hour later, when Tessie arrived with her loom in the back of a pickup, Anna was already excited about the results of her work. She'd found some old crockery in the kitchen and placed a poinsettia plant in each one. Then she lined them up on the stairway. The ruby glassware shone in the windows and on the mantel, and she'd arranged fir boughs and red velvet ribbon around the glassware.

Tessie arrived with an armload of fresh holly wrapped in wax paper.

"Wonderful!" Anna exclaimed.

"I sprinkled it down, and I'd keep it in water until a day or so before the filming," Tessie advised. "Nothing looks worse than dried-out holly."

"It'll be the perfect final touch." Anna took the bundle into the kitchen and found a large mason jar to fill with water. "I sure appreciate this."

"And I sure appreciate all the yarn you've been buying, even when your loom is in New York," Tessie said as she followed her into the kitchen. "You didn't need to do that."

"Sure I did. Your coaching has helped me through some tough projects this fall, and besides, you agreed to bring your loom over this week so that I could have the other one in the city." She set the holly in a corner of the kitchen. "I'll get my coat and help you carry it in."

Tessie was prepared with a ramp, as Sam had been,

and the two women unloaded the loom with no trouble.

"You've got a holiday project on this loom," Anna said, feeling guilty. "I shouldn't deprive you of time to work right before Christmas."

"That project is there for a reason. I thought you'd want the loom to seem as if it's in use, so I started a red, white and green tablecloth I've been wanting to make every Christmas for five years." She grinned. "I'll write down the treadling, and you can work on it whenever you want this week."

"In my free time," Anna said, chuckling as she glanced at the open boxes and bags strewn around the parlor.

"Looks like you're getting a handle on it," Tessie said. "Oh, I almost forgot. In the seat of the truck I have another accessory I thought you'd like. Be right back." She returned quickly with a rattan basket filled with skeins of red, white and green yarn. "You can set this next to the loom, maybe."

"Definitely," Anna said, placing the basket on the floor to one side of the loom. "That looks terrific. Tessie, you have quite an eye. Ever thought of interior design?"

"Sure. But I like it in Sumersbury, so I run a yarn shop, instead."

Anna nodded. "Point taken." She picked up a green satin ribbon from the box on the sofa and absently wound it around her finger. "Sam would like me to move here permanently, to be with him, of course, but also because he thinks I'd love it."

"Maybe you would."

"Maybe." She pulled the ribbon tight. "But I'd have to give up interior design."

"And become a weaver, like Hilary?" Tessie smiled.

"Sam likes to think that, but I—I don't know."

Tessie surveyed the room thoughtfully for a while. "I remember what this room looked like when Hilary was alive," she said. "She may have shared your talent for weaving, but not for this sort of work. The place looks fantastic."

"Thank you," Anna said, surprised and complimented.

"If this is an example of what you can do, I...." Tessie glanced away.

"What?"

"It's none of my business. This is between you and Sam." She gazed at Anna and laughed softly. "That's what comes of living in a small town too long. You really begin to think you should mind everyone else's business for them."

"Tessie, you've been a friend to me and I don't consider you a meddling person. I cherish your advice. Please finish what you were about to say."

Tessie hesitated. "I just think you should be careful about discarding something you do so well. Sam's wonderful. He's one of my favorite people in Sumersbury. But this—" She waved her hand around the room. "You have a gift for this. Since you've been foolish enough to beg my opinion, I'd advise you to find a way to have the man and the career."

Anna shook her head. "I doubt if that would fit Sam's rural fantasy for us."

"So expand his horizons."

Anna thought about that for a moment. "Or mine," she said. "Maybe I have an even greater gift for weaving. Maybe it's time for a change in my life, a settling down to a quieter time, to thoughts of a family. I'm almost thirty, Tessie."

"You see?" Tessie smiled and held up both hands. "You could take my advice and be furious because I convinced you to give up your country idyll, where you would have been much happier than slaving away in the city. Forget what I said. What do I know?"

"I'll bet you know how to decorate a Christmas tree."

"I've managed a few in my time. This one?"

"No, Sam and I will tackle that tonight, with his family ornaments. But I have to do some creative things with the others."

"Others?"

"This is a Christmas-tree farm," Anna said, laughing. "We have one in every room, even the bathroom."

"Good grief."

"So I thought if I bribed you with a cup of hot coffee you might help me."

Tessie shrugged. "Why not? I closed the shop early today because, starting Monday, I won't have a break until Christmas Eve."

"Meaning I won't get you over here again all week?"

"That's right. You're on your own, unless you'd like to call Estelle for a coffee klatch."

"I'm coming to appreciate Estelle's admirable qualities, but no thanks. Anyway, it'll be good for me to fend for myself this week. I can really test this country living."

"That's what this week is, then?" Tessie lifted her pale eyebrows.

"Yep."

"You're not so dumb, after all," Tessie said. "Let's go make that coffee and then we'll trim your trees. I vote we begin with the one in the bathroom. I've never decorated a bathroom Christmas tree, and I love new experiences."

AT NINE THAT NIGHT the last buyers left, an eight-foot spruce tied to the luggage rack on top of their station wagon. All of Sam's helpers, including John, had gone home to their families around seven, but a persistent trickle of customers had kept Sam outside for another two hours.

He came in the back door stomping his feet from the cold. Either a woodpecker was loose in the house orAnna was pounding in nails, he thought, listening to the erratic tapping noise. "Anna?" He loved being able to call her name when he came in from the day's work.

The tapping stopped. "In here," she called from the parlor.

He took off his gloves and stuffed them into the pockets of his jacket before taking it off and hooking it over the peg by the door. Despite the sheepskin gloves, his hands felt like ice. He blew on them as he walked through the house to find her.

She was balanced on a step ladder, hanging gingerbread cookies from the beams while a fire crackled on the grate. Firelight danced in her hair, making it seem to curl down her back like flame. He wondered how he'd ever enjoyed this house without her in it. "The place looks fantastic already," he said when she turned to smile at him.

"No more customers?"

"If they show up, we're not answering the door. Anybody who wants a tree this time of night can get it somewhere else."

"I'm almost finished with these, and then we can have some soup and toasted cheese sandwiches, if that sounds okay."

"Lady, anything you suggest sound okay with me. Need any help with that?" He was torn between wanting to haul her off the ladder for a kiss and wanting to watch her earnestly decorating his home. Their home someday, he hoped.

"I'll just be a minute," she said, rapping a finishing nail into the heavy beam. Soon a gingerbread Santa dangled from the beam, suspended by a red ribbon. "A couple more and I'll quit," she added.

"In the meantime I'll go upstairs and wash some of this grit off," he said, thinking that a quick shower might be in order after the day he'd put in and the night he had in mind.

"Take a look around while you're up there," she called when he reached the landing. "Tessie and I accomplished a lot before she left this afternoon."

Before he stripped for his shower he did as Anna suggested and was entranced by the effect she and Tessie had created. During the original redecorating, Anna had given one of the two small bedrooms a feminine look and the other a masculine one. "I know it's stereotyped," she'd said, "and if there were real kids in these rooms I might not be this heavy-handed, but for the cameras it will be fun."

Her reference to "real kids" in those rooms had made his gut twist with desire for the family he craved, but he hadn't let on. Instead he'd admired her choice of a white eyelet spread for the girl's room and a bold red-white-and-blue pattern for the boy's room. She'd borrowed some old dolls from her friend Vivian and these sat in a rocker in the girl's room. The phantom boy possessed Sam's toy airplane and his cherished fire truck, both displayed on an old leather trunk.

Sam paused in the hall outside the boy's room, the room that had, in fact, been his while his grandparents were still alive. A multicolored glow lit the room, and he remembered with a sweet pang that his grandparents had put a tree in his bedroom the years he'd been at the farm for Christmas and he'd drifted off to sleep each night with that same gentle rainbow washing the room.

He stepped inside to savor the memories. The four-foot tree in the corner was decorated with toy-shaped wooden ornaments and lots of candy canes. Because the ornaments followed a theme, the final effect was more professional than anything his grandmother had ever created, and therefore less personal, too, but Sam loved the room anyway. All it lacked was a boy, a son—his and Anna's. He wondered if she'd considered that, even a little, while she worked on this room.

The girl's room twinkled, with miniature white lights scattered over the tree like stardust. For decorations Anna had wound a garland of lace around the branches and fastened a bevy of pink bows at the tips. Sam easily imagined a little girl with strawberry curls asleep beneath the eyelet.

Even though he wasn't personally eager for the television crews to arrive, Sam looked forward to showing off Anna's work. He regretted that the filming was scheduled for daytime, because the real magic of these rooms came through now, when the tree lights were the only illumination in the soft darkness. During the day the lights wouldn't show up at all, something Anna must have realized. She could have eliminated lights from all the extra trees.

He walked into the master bedroom, thinking about that as he admired the blue-and-gold beauty of a pine, all eight feet of it, that greeted him there. Sexy, he thought, but she could have left the lights off this one, too. The blue and gold ornaments picked up the colors of the quilt, the woven blanket and the plaid armchair and ottoman. All of that was logical, but why had she gone the extra mile with blue lights?

The only possible answer was a desire to reach beyond the requirements of the television special and decorate for him. Sam liked that explanation, and he whistled as he took a shower in the bathroom. He left the overhead switch off and soaped himself in the cheerful glow of red lights wound around a tiny live tree sitting in a redwood pot by the bathtub.

When he came downstairs again he complimented Anna on the job she'd done in the bedrooms and bath, but he didn't raise the subject of the lights until later, when they began the task of decorating the ten-foot tree in the parlor.

"You realize the filming in the house will be during the day," he said casually as he climbed the stepladder with a strand of lights for the top portion of the tree.

"Yes, I know."

"So for the special, tree lights aren't really necessary, I suppose."

"True, but you want them for yourself, don't you? Especially on this one."

"Yes, I do," he said, gazing down at her with a

smile. "I love the lights on all the trees, and I felt as if they were turned on just for me when I went up there tonight. Thank you, Anna."

She flushed a delicious pink. "I guess the professional designer got carried away. I knew the lights weren't necessary, but I also knew how the rooms could look at night if the trees had them. The expense wasn't much, so I did it."

"For me," he said softly.

She nodded.

He gazed down at her. "How I love you, Anna Tilford."

"I love you, too."

"Let's trim the tree tomorrow night," he said, backing down the ladder.

"But I thought you wanted—"

"I want you out of those clothes and covered with blue light," he said, putting the strand he'd been holding on the floor and guiding her toward the stairway. "I want to make love to you in the glow from a Christmas tree, and this one will take far too long to decorate."

"I've been picturing you in blue light, too," she acknowledged with a smile.

To his delight, once they'd undressed and thrown the covers back on the sleigh bed, she took the initiative, kneeling above him to offer a taste of her breasts. He captured the swaying nipple greedily and tugged a moan from her lips as he applied gentle suction. Meanwhile he roamed her body with eager hands, sculpting her waist, her hips and the seductive triangle that brushed so tantalizingly, yet wouldn't settle, wouldn't allow him to find her soft center.

Twice he'd reached for the package beside the bed, and twice she'd caught his hand. "Not yet," she murmured.

He cradled the weight of her breasts, damp from his lips and tongue, and admired their graceful curve outlined in the blue glow from the tree. The light made her look unreal, a creature from his lusty imagination, a mythical woman who appeared like magic in his bed.

The fantasy continued as she kissed her way from his throat to his chest, from his belly to the focus point of all sensation. He gave himself up to the ecstasy created by this blue goddess with the clever lips and tongue. He might become addicted to blue light, he thought as she drove him to the edge of control.

When he thought he could stand no more, she reached for the package herself, and quicker than he could have imagined, she took care of everything and moved astride him. He gazed with rapture at the play of blue across her undulating body as she loved him. The view was terrific, and he realized what he sacrificed every time she was under him and blocked by his shadow and weight.

"I love you in blue," he said, grasping her rolling hips and urging her to a faster pace.

"And I...just plain...love you," she whispered, taking her cue and giving him the increased friction he sought.

The dream quality of the blue light combined with her sensuous rhythm to snap his control. He dug his fingers into her soft flesh as spasms rocked him and he gasped out her name. *This is forever*. The thought streaked across his heated mind like a comet while her cries of completion rained down on him. *This is forever*.

As he gathered her close in the shuddering aftermath of passion, he vowed to break the silence about marriage very soon. Once the craziness of this week was over, he'd ask her to be his wife, to live with him in Sumersbury and fill the two bedrooms with children born of his love for her. He could see no other future for him but that. No other options made sense.

12

ANNA HAD OVERESTIMATED the time she'd need to decorate Sam's house *and* how much time Sam would have for her. The phone rang constantly during the day as she fielded calls from Estelle and other townspeople. In addition, staff members from the White House called regarding Sam's tea with the First Lady, an honor he'd received in exchange for providing the White House tree. The television network also relayed messages through Anna. Unfortunately, playing receptionist wasn't her favorite role.

Sam took his few spare moments to return the calls, including one to his mother, who was furious that she and her husband were forced to stay at a nearby inn instead of Sam's house. When Anna had asked if his mother and her husband should be allowed to use the two twin beds upstairs, Sam had explained that his mother wasn't a careful guest and might ruin the effect Anna had worked so hard to create. His mother's only motivation, Sam had said, was to increase her chance of jumping in front of the television camera.

Anna fussed with the house as much as she dared, adding candle arrangements, wreaths and garlands until she feared overdoing the decoration. She completed a large part of Tessie's tablecloth project on the loom, and she even approached John about helping to cut and stack Christmas trees.

"Hell, no!" John had boomed out, picking up a wrapped tree and tossing it onto a stack in the barn. "Sam said this is your vacation, or it's supposed to be. You had to decorate the house and all, even so. Relax, girl! Take a walk. Read a book. Watch television. And if you're really lookin' for somethin' to do, pray for snow."

Anna had never been much of a television watcher, and she couldn't seem to concentrate on reading. So she'd taken walks along the country lane or sat on a rock wall and thought. She had no faith that she could make it snow, so that part of John's suggestion had gone unheeded.

She'd hated to admit boredom to herself, much less to Sam. Every evening he'd looked so happy to see her there, waiting to share a late supper and tales of his day. But he'd been too tired for the games of Parcheesi and Kentucky Derby they'd promised each other they'd play.

In their conversations she'd tried to sound cheerful and busy and hadn't mentioned how she itched to work on the design projects she had under contract in the city. She also hadn't told him about her impulses during the day to call Vivian long-distance at the store, just to hear her sassy, big-city accent.

When she'd been in Sam's arms, making love in the sleigh bed, she'd forgotten the store and her clients, the thrill of completing a difficult assignment and the challenge of budgets and unusual tastes. But when he hadn't been with her, the house had been empty and quiet, far too quiet. Anna had even begun to miss the honking taxicabs.

She was demented, she thought. Any normal person would relish a chance to live in the healthful environment of Sumersbury, away from noise and car exhaust and buildings that blocked the sun. Yet all those things were a part of the excitement she craved. Not that she didn't love the country, too. She did. She wanted both.

The snow began at noon on Thursday, and the people of Sumersbury acted as if the sky had filled with dollar bills. In a way it had, Anna realized, because now the tree cutting ceremony had a real chance of looking the way everyone in town hoped it would. Sam reported that the pond was freezing fast. By five o'clock, tree cutting operations were ended because of the snow.

No one came to buy trees that night as the snow fell thick and fast, but that didn't free Sam to spend time with Anna. The telephone rang constantly. It seemed everyone involved in Saturday's event required personal reassurance that everything was under control.

The townspeople wouldn't be called upon until Saturday, but Sam had to face the cameras on Friday afternoon, when the interior of the house would be filmed. Friday evening, Sam's mother and stepfather would arrive in Sumersbury and so would Anna's friends Vivian and Jimmy. The extravaganza was about to begin.

As they climbed the stairs to bed, Sam and Anna were both edgy, he from the tension of the approaching event and she from a dawning realization that she couldn't be a full-time country girl. Their lovemaking that night reflected their uneasiness.

"It'll be better after this is all over," Sam told her as they both tried to shake off their individual cares and concentrate on each other. "What we need is some peace and quiet."

A denial was on Anna's lips, but she kissed him instead of speaking. Now wasn't the moment for her to reveal her uncertainties about their future together. The next two days would be stressful enough without adding that to the mix.

FRIDAY PASSED IN A BLUR. Snow had fallen all through the night and well into the morning, and snowplows worked ceaselessly to keep the roads clear. John spent the morning atop Sam's tractor plow, and by noon he had both the driveway and the road up to the tree site passable.

No sooner had he finished than television crews arrived in a van equipped as a mobile station. As the van parked in front of the house, Anna beat a quick retreat to the barn, where John was putting away the tractor.

"What's the matter? Don't you wanna be on TV?"

he asked with a grin as he climbed down from the tractor seat.

"Absolutely not. Besides, everyone who watches this special is supposed to think Sam decorated the house, or if not Sam, then some loving, motherly type who's taken this poor boy under her wing."

John glanced at her. "Guess you don't fit that picture."

Anna met his assessing gaze and wondered if John had figured out more than Sam had about this relationship. "No, John, I don't," she agreed as they walked outside together. "I'm what they call a career woman, I guess."

"Nothin' wrong with that." John scooped snow from a drift beside the barn and molded it between his gloved hands.

"There is if I want to settle down in Sumersbury. I don't think Sam would like me to commute back and forth."

"Maybe not, but it's your work, not his." He threw the snowball, which hit the side of the van with a splat.

"John," Anna reprimanded with a chuckle. "I think someone's in there monitoring the equipment. What will they think?"

John shrugged and grinned at her. "That not everybody in Sumersbury is crazy about this TV special idea."

"Oh." Anna laughed with him. "Listen, you have a point about my work. I hope Sam agrees with you."

"If he doesn't, he's a damned fool, and I'd tell him so to his face, too."

"I'll bet you would. And thanks for the vote of confidence, John." Anna started to walk away but paused as a long white car drove in and parked next to the van. "What's with the limo?"

"That's probably the guy who's gonna narrate the special. He plays the father in that family TV show, the one with the four kids, and the wife's a stockbroker. You know the one I mean? Tuesday nights it's on."

"I don't watch much TV."

"Well, anyway, it's him. Take my word for it. Tomorrow everybody'll be scrambling for autographs."

"John, do you think we'll all make it through tomorrow without a major disaster?"

John scratched behind his ear and glanced at the van and the limo. "If you ask me, the disaster's already happened. All that's left is to see if it gets worse."

AT TEN THE NEXT MORNING, Anna stood with Vivian and Jimmy behind the rock wall that divided Sam's property from the road. They'd tramped a path for themselves to this vantage point for viewing the parade, complete with Santa Claus, that Estelle had arranged.

Sam's mother and stepfather sat in wooden chairs on the front porch, drinking coffee. When they'd discovered they would have to walk instead of ride to the tree site, they'd elected to stay on the porch. Sam's mother was also miffed that the interior of the house had been filmed before she'd arrived. Anna hadn't been able to coax much friendliness from her, so finally she'd given up and suggested to Jimmy and Vivian that the view would be better nearer the road.

Finally, fifteen minutes later than scheduled, the strange procession appeared in the distance. In the lead was the television van, a cameraman sprawled on its roof while he trained his lens back down the road. Behind the van came Santa in his sleigh pulled by the pet doe.

When they drew closer, Anna could tell that the doe's transformation into Rudolph had been less than a success. The horns kept sliding sideways, and Santa had to leap out of his sleigh every few seconds, shout "Cut!" and reposition the antlers. Anna wondered if the cameraman listened to Santa's filming directives.

Trailing the sleigh was a pickup with Estelle Terwiliger, swathed in imitation ermine and looking like a polar bear, enthroned in the back. With wide, sweeping motions she directed the Sumersbury Town Choir marching behind her. A second cameraman walked backward next to the truck and alternately swung his camera from Estelle to the choir singing "O Come, All Ye Faithful."

Estelle's fur-covered rump rested uneasily on the seat of a carved wooden chair that Anna suspected had been liberated from the pulpit of a local church.

Her bouncing came partly from the bumpy road and partly from the energetic way she directed the choir.

"Holy Toledo," Vivian whispered as Estelle's conducting lifted her several inches from her seat. "With arm motions like that, she could part the Red Sea."

"I imagine Estelle could part the Red Sea if she cared to," Anna replied. "She's quite a woman."

"And besides all this, there's an orchestra up on the hill and a pond with costumed skaters?" Jimmy asked.

"That's right," Anna confirmed. "Sam and John took three loads of kids up in the back of the truck this morning. They were all in position by nine-thirty, including Sam and John at the tree site."

Vivian nudged Anna in the ribs. "Is this supposed to be funny? You didn't tell us it was supposed to be funny."

"It's not," Anna replied. "But Sam figured all along that it would be."

"Sam's a yummy guy, Anna."

"And Vivian knows yummy when she sees it," Jimmy added, grinning.

"Right, Jimmy-boy." Vivian linked her arm through her husband's and gave a squeeze. "Whoops, there go the antlers sliding off again. I guess that red blinking thing under the deer's chin was supposed to be Rudolph's nose, huh?"

"Yes," Anna said. "There's a wire running along the bridle and back to a battery pack in the sleigh."

Vivian peered at the white-bearded man in the

sleigh. "Do you know who's playing Santa? He's definitely got the belly for it, unless those are pillows."

Anna smiled. "Those aren't pillows. Santa is Edgar Madison, who's known for staying drunk between Thanksgiving and Christmas. Estelle gave him the role of Santa in exchange for a pledge to stay sober for the holidays this year. I guess she didn't want the TV cameras to catch him staggering down the main street of town today."

"The temperance movement is alive in Sumersbury," Vivian said, rolling her eyes. "I hope that poor deer won't have to pull chubby Edgar up the hill to the ceremony, though."

"No." Anna watched the doe's patient trek along the road. "Santa and the sleigh will stay here, in Sam's yard." She noticed Tessie in the choir and waved. Then she looked for Daphne Michaels and was relieved not to find Sam's old girlfriend in the crowd. Sam had mentioned that Daphne might be ticked off at him and wouldn't show up today, regardless of the event.

Anna's thoughts were interrupted as Estelle picked up a bullhorn and bellowed out, "'O Holy Night'! On the downbeat!"

"Cut!" cried Santa, leaping from the sleigh to right Rudolph's antlers once more.

The cameraman swung his lens toward Estelle, and she must have seen him do it, Anna thought, because she bellowed out a second command. "Give it all you've got, choir!" she shouted, and in her enthusiasm stood with both arms raised.

The move wasn't wise. The pickup hit a bump in the road, and Estelle tumbled to the bed of the truck. Members of the choir rushed forward to help her, but the driver, unaware that his charge was crawling on her hands and knees in the back, kept driving.

Eventually he heard the shouting from the choir and stopped. Estelle regained her seat, although the imitation ermine was smudged and the hat askew. She retrieved the bullhorn and directed it toward the front of the parade. "Are the antlers ready, Edgar?" she called.

"Antlers ready!" pronounced Santa, climbing into his sleigh.

"'O Holy Night'!" Estelle repeated into the bullhorn. "On the downbeat!"

Vivian couldn't control her giggles, and she hid her face in Jimmy's shoulder until she was calmer. "I will cancel any and all my social plans when this airs," she said to Anna. "Wild horses couldn't drag me away from my television set that night. And we haven't even gotten to the skaters and the orchestra yet."

"The government guys seem unfazed by this," Jimmy remarked, tilting his head toward a gray sedan where two hatless men in topcoats and business suits leaned against the fender. "Every once in a while they crack a smile, but that's about it."

"They've seen crazier stunts than this in their day,

I'll bet," Vivian said. "Hanging around the White House probably blunts you to all other forms of entertainment."

Anna laughed. "I've missed you, Viv."

"Have you? I find that hard to believe with an entertaining fellow like Sam Garrison around."

"Oh, don't get me wrong. Sam's wonderful, but I like being with you sometimes, too."

"Spoken like a true friend. Jimmy and I will make every effort to visit you when you settle into this rural utopia." She smiled at Anna before returning her attention to the parade. "Ah, the sleigh's turning in the driveway. That poor creature will get its rest at last."

"Vivian, who mentioned anything about my settling down here?" Anna said.

"Nobody, but I can't imagine why not," Vivian replied, still watching the parade. "You and Sam are bonkers about each other, and marriage is a wonderful institution for people in your condition."

"Yes, but—"

"Never mind that now," Vivian said. "We're following the choir up the hill, right? I don't want to miss a single bit of this. Will the cameras pick us out, do you think, way in the back?"

Jimmy took her hand as they started off. "Viv, I expect you'll have a contract with Warner Brothers a week after this special runs."

"You're just saying that because I'm so photogenic," Vivian said, laughing. "Come along, Anna.

We'll talk about your love life when this is over, I promise."

With Santa out of the parade, the second cameraman climbed back into the van and let his partner on the roof finish the coverage of the trek up the hillside. As the pickup lurched upward, Estelle steadied herself with one hand on the tailgate and directed with the hand that held the bullhorn. Periodically she brought the bullhorn to her mouth and commanded, "Louder! With more joy!"

"Easy for her to say," panted Vivian, who had decided to join in the singing, too. "She's riding on a frigging truck. How much farther, Anna?"

"I'm not sure. The last time I came up here, I was riding in a truck, too."

"I'm not cut out for this," Vivian complained, sagging dramatically against Jimmy. "Carry me, Jimmyboy. Pretend you're Rhett Butler and I'm Scarlett O'Hara."

"I have a better idea," Jimmy said, propping her upright. "Let's pretend we're Butch Cassidy and the Sundance Kid robbing a train, and we'll leap aboard that truck with what's-her-name."

"Estelle Terwiliger," Anna said, laughing breathlessly as she trudged beside them. "That's what we get for being city slickers who don't get enough exercise."

"We could turn back," Jimmy suggested hopefully.

"Not on your life," Vivian retorted. "If you won't carry me, I may have to crawl up this hill, but I'm not missing the pond and the skaters and the felling of a mighty oak."

"Fir," Jimmy corrected.

"Right. Fir. I'm going on. I'll take a bath in Ben-Gay tonight."

"I'm going, too. I certainly can't miss this," Anna said. "Besides, the pond's just ahead," she added, peering around the jumble of choir members trying valiantly to sing and march going uphill. "I think I hear the orchestra playing 'The Skaters' Waltz.'"

"If you two women can make it, so can I," Jimmy pledged.

They reached the clearing, and Estelle chopped off the end of the Christmas carol with one clean swipe of her arm. Then she rose from her chair and regally turned to watch the skaters on the pond she'd ordered up from Sam.

Anna and her friends couldn't see very well, and apparently neither could the choir members, who broke ranks and surged around the truck to get a better view. The cleared portion of the narrow road was clogged with the television van, Estelle's truck and the town choir.

"Jimmy, help me up onto your shoulders," Vivian demanded, hopping up and down trying to see over everyone's head. "I'll miss it."

"My shoulders?" Jimmy stared at her. "Anna's friend Sam is the one with the shoulders, Viv. I'm a poor office worker, remember?"

"Don't be silly," Vivian said. "I'm not overweight

and you're stronger than you think. Kneel down and let me climb on."

Anna smothered her laughter as Vivian straddled Jimmy's neck and he grasped her boot-clad ankles before staggering to his feet with a groan.

"Oh, you should see this!" Vivian exclaimed from her wobbly perch.

"Thanks, Viv," Jimmy replied. "I'd love to. Maybe you could hold me on your shoulders. I'm not overweight and you're stronger than you think you are," he added, weaving a little as he fought to keep his footing on the slushy road.

"What's it look like?" Anna asked, craning her neck.

"Would you like to climb onto Vivian's shoulders?" Jimmy asked, grimacing as his wife shifted her weight. "I saw that in the circus once. I'll bet we could get on TV if I held both of you up at once."

"Jimmy, don't be ridiculous," Vivian said. "You're such a baby. Move a little to the right, so I can— There! A perfect view. Oh, they're so cute!"

"Color commentary, if you please, Viv," Jimmy prodded, "for the rabble here below you. 'Cute' doesn't provide a very clear picture."

"Well, the girls have on long skirts and fur hats, and they're holding little muffs. The boys aren't fixed up too different from the way boys dress today, except they have on those little flat caps like golfers sometimes wear and bright scarfs. The orchestra must be like ice cubes, though. Those poor kids' lips and fingers look blue, even from here."

"But they sound pretty good," Anna said. "I'm glad that something went as planned, for a change, and—"

"Oh, no!" Vivian exclaimed. "Oh, dear! Whoops, there goes another one."

"What?" Anna and Jimmy begged together.

"Oh, those poor kids. They're not used to skating with long skirts. Look out!"

"Ouch, Viv," Jimmy cried. "Let go of my hair!"

"Just like dominoes!" Vivian wailed.

"Vivian," Jimmy said, "stop bouncing around, or—"

"Steady, Jimmy," Anna cautioned. He listed toward a snowbank, and Anna hurried forward to help, but Jimmy's momentum carried all three of them along as Vivian began to shriek. Arms and legs flailing, they landed in four feet of snow, which cushioned the fall but covered them from head to foot in wet flakes.

After a moment of silence, Jimmy's string of mumbled curses told Anna he was all right, and Vivian began to laugh. Anna looked at her two friends, hair and eyebrows covered with snow, and she began to laugh, too.

Then she realized that the orchestra was no longer playing. She turned slowly and discovered a camera pointed directly at her and the entire Sumersbury Town Choir standing in a semicircle behind the cameraman. Still laughing, Anna picked up a handful of snow and flung it toward the camera.

Jimmy took his cue and made a snowball, but his aim was off and he hit one of the men of the choir. The fellow grinned and raced for the edge of the road, where he made his own snowball. With a whoop, Vivian jumped into the fray, and before long everyone except Estelle Terwiliger was laughing and throwing snowballs. The cameraman, caught in the cross fire, retreated to his van while Estelle brayed for order through her bullhorn.

"Stop! Stop this minute!" shouted Estelle, dodging incoming snowballs. Nobody stopped. "Behave yourselves!" she bellowed. No response. "What about the tree?" she screamed at last, and slowly everyone grew still and smiled sheepishly at one another. "That's better," Estelle announced. "Now, sopranos over here, tenors there. Altos and basses, you know your places."

"Hey, that rhymes," Vivian whispered to Jimmy.

"I'd be quiet if I were you," he mumbled back. "You've already caused enough trouble."

"Me? Anna fired the first shot." Vivian punched Anna playfully on the arm. "I didn't think you had it in you."

Jimmy glanced at Anna and smiled. "You did start that whole thing, come to think of it."

"I guess I did." Anna chuckled and brushed the snow from her coat. The choir was reassembled, and with another command from Estelle, they launched into "Silent Night" and began marching up the road again. "It was fun, too," Anna admitted under cover of the singing.

"I do declare," Vivian said as they trudged along behind the choir, "you're turning into one spunky gal, Anna Tilford. I'm proud of you."

"Thanks."

As the procession went by the pond, teenagers with skates over their shoulders or instrument cases in one hand hurried to join the choir. Anna was close enough to hear when a boy in braces spoke to a woman in the back of the choir.

"Mom, did you guys really have a snowball fight back there?" the boy asked between verses of the Christmas carol. "Somebody said you had a snowball fight on camera."

"We did." The woman sounded proud of herself.

"And I thought we were bad, having that pileup on the ice. Did you see that?"

"Some. I guess the poor girls should have practiced with those skirts before today."

"Will they show that on TV, Mom?" the boy asked anxiously. "If they do, I'll be pretty embarrassed."

His mother laughed. "Listen, son. On the way up here, the reindeer's antlers slid off about forty times, and the red nose never did work right. Estelle Terwiliger fell down in the bed of the truck. Then you and the rest of the skaters turned into a pile of pick-up sticks, and the choir got into a snowball fight." She laughed again. "We're putting on a terrific show. I wouldn't be surprised if the whole town got invited on Johnny Carson. Now let's sing."

Anna smiled to herself. A year ago she never would have thrown that handful of snow at the cameraman. She wouldn't have taken her nighttime hike over the path, either, or suggested using her own weavings in a client's decor. She was becoming her own person at last.

The procession reached the tall fir trees near the spot where the White House tree grew. Up the road Anna glimpsed Sam's battered truck and a gleaming red truck-and-trailer combination that he'd rented to transport the tree to Washington. A tractor and a large sled would bring the tree to the road once it was felled. Sam had described the whole process to her.

The television van pulled to the far left of the road and stopped behind Sam's truck.

The driver of Estelle's pickup braked just behind the van, and Estelle spoke into the bullhorn. "The television crew will stay here, and a cameraman will be allowed near the tree site for the cutting ceremony," she said. "We will proceed up the road a bit and be able to see some of the action from there. As I explained to all of you before, we can't stand around and watch the tree fall. Someone might get hurt."

"I wonder where she got that idea," Jimmy said. "It's not as if this whole thing hasn't been a series of pratfalls already. All we need is to crush a few people under the White House Christmas tree to make the day complete."

"I think it's been great," Vivian said. "Even if I'm wet and cold and I'll have to use a wheelchair to get through the next week, I don't regret a minute."

"Follow me, choir members," Estelle said through the bullhorn. The truck eased to the right of the van.

"Is there enough room for Estelle's truck to get by?" Anna wondered out loud.

As if in answer, the truck tilted to the right and stalled. Estelle screamed, but she didn't fall this time. She recovered quickly, glanced nervously at the television van, where a grinning cameraman was pointing his camera straight at her, and raised the bullhorn to her lips. "Would the male members of the choir please assist us out of this ditch?" she asked calmly.

Everyone laughed, and the men and boys put their shoulders into the job while the cameras rolled. The truck's tires spun slush and mud over everyone in the general vicinity, but nobody seemed to care anymore. Soon the truck was free, and the choir, no longer looking the least angelic, burst into "Hark, the Herald Angels Sing" with no prompting from Estelle.

"There's Sam!" Vivian called to Anna as they passed the row where the White House tree stood. "He's with that TV star. Frankly, I think Sam is better looking."

Anna had already noticed Sam and John in conversation with the television personality and two more representatives from the White House. Sam glanced her way, and her newfound confidence allowed her to wave at him. He smiled and waved back, causing

Anna's heart to lurch with pride. The man she loved was providing a Christmas tree that the president and his family would enjoy all season and thousands of visitors to the capital would admire, as well.

"Oh, Anna, the look on your face gives you away," Vivian teased. "You'd better marry that boy."

"I guess I'd better," she agreed, waving at him once more before following the choir and Estelle up the hill a few more yards. "If he'll have me."

"Are you kidding?" Vivian hooted. "He's stepped into the cow patty of love with both feet."

Jimmy snorted. "I've got to get you out of the country, Viv. You're lapsing into some really strange expressions."

Estelle stood in the back of the pickup. "Now everyone turn around and watch," she instructed. "When the tree crashes down, I want the orchestra to accompany me on the 'Ave Maria.'"

"Lord, she's really going to do it," Anna whispered to Vivian and Jimmy.

"You mean sing?" Jimmy asked in a low voice. "Why shouldn't she?"

"According to Sam, her singing is like raccoons mating," Anna replied softly.

A chain saw fired up, and a hush settled over the choir. Anna could tell which tree was being cut when its top began to quiver. "There," she said to Vivian and Jimmy, pointing.

"This is really neat," Vivian said, slipping her arm

through Jimmy's. "The White House tree being cut, and we were there."

"Yeah, thanks, Anna," Jimmy said, putting an arm around Anna's shoulders and giving her a hug. "Thanks for putting up with us this weekend."

"I'm glad you're here," Anna said, meaning it completely. She hadn't been able to be with Sam much, but her friends were important, too, she realized. Besides, Sam had been quite busy the past twenty-four hours with his mother and stepfather, anyway.

The teenage boy in braces hurried over to them. "When it goes, we're all going to yell 'Timber!'" he whispered. "We passed the word around the choir."

"Does Estelle know?" Anna whispered back.

"No, but don't you think it's a perfect thing to do?"

Vivian patted the boy on the shoulder. "Absolutely. Thanks for letting us in on it."

The boy hurried back to his spot, the tree wobbled, and as the top branches disappeared, the choir shouted "Timber!" and threw their hands in the air.

Estelle jumped at the unexpected reaction, but she had no time to think about it because the orchestra launched immediately into the "Ave Maria." Taking a deep breath, Estelle Terwiliger began to sing through the bullhorn.

13

SAM WAS SCHEDULED to leave for Washington that same afternoon so the tree would arrive as fresh as possible. The television crew stayed in town for one last shot of the famous fir departing Sumersbury. Sam had promised the merchants he'd drive down the main street, and every able-bodied person for miles around planned to be on the sidewalk waving as he passed in the red truck and trailer.

Vivian and Jimmy had gone into town to explore and be on hand for the sidewalk waving campaign, as had Sam's mother and stepfather. Sam had asked Anna to stay and talk to him while he made last-minute preparations for the trip, and she'd grabbed the chance to be alone with him before they were separated again.

"What a day this has been, huh?" he said, taking the stairs to his bedroom quickly. Since yesterday he'd moved and talked faster than before, but Anna figured anybody in Sam's position would be wired. "I just have a few more things to throw into the suitcase," he added over his shoulder, "and I wanted your advice about which suit to wear for the White House tea next Wednesday."

She followed him up the stairs, her step slower than his. She was amazed to discover that his celebrity status made her shy with him, even here, in this bedroom where they'd shared such intimacy. "I think the filming went pretty well, all things considered," she said.

He glanced up from the suitcase lying open on the sleigh bed. "Yeah," he said, chuckling, "all things considered. When I heard Estelle's 'Ave Maria' coming over that bullhorn, I just about croaked. You should have seen the expression on Dev's face."

"'Dev'?"

He took two shirts from the refinished dresser and tucked them into the suitcase. "The guy from the TV series. You know, Devlin Maxwell."

"Oh, yes, of course."

"So which one should I take?" he asked, hurrying to the closet and pulling out two suits.

Anna stared at the gray and dark blue three-piece suits, both well cut and expensive looking. "Do you know I've never seen you in a suit?"

"You won't catch me wearing one any more than I have to, either. This is an honor and everything, but I can't wait for things to get back to normal around here."

"I'd take the dark blue," Anna said.

"Yeah, I think so, too." He returned to the closet for a garment bag and hung the suit inside it. "You know, Anna, getting caught up in this frantic pace reminds me how much I hate it." He zipped the garment bag and laid it next to the suitcase on the bed.

Anna had nothing to say. She sensed that he wanted her to agree that frantic was bad and quiet was good. She couldn't.

"Anna?" He walked around the bed and took her in his arms. "Listen, I know the past two days have been a mess, and we've hardly had any time together. I wish you could go to Washington with me. Is there any way? We could buy you some clothes once we got there, and—"

She pressed her fingertips gently against his lips and shook her head. "I've just had a week off, Sam. Several of my clients want their design projects done before Christmas, and I have a billion things to do. I'd love to be with you, but I can't afford to take another week."

He rubbed her back and sighed. "Sometimes I curse myself for not getting to know you when you first moved in. If we'd met at the beginning of the summer, instead of at the end, I'll bet you wouldn't be at that job right now."

She stared at him and her stomach began to churn. "Sam, I—"

"I know. I know." He cupped her face with one hand. "You can't march in there and give them your resignation in the middle of the Christmas rush. But Anna, it's got to happen sooner or later. We both know that. You belong here with me, not slaving away in that madhouse they call New York. Look at how depressed you're acting, knowing your week is over and you have to go back there tomorrow."

Anna trembled as she sensed the approaching storm. She should have seen it coming and diverted the conversation. Instead, she'd been lost in her own thoughts about this very subject, and Sam had misinterpreted her silence. The timing was lousy, but she couldn't allow him to misunderstand any longer. She gazed deep into his blue eyes. "Sam, I love you, and I love being with you."

"Same here. That's why—"

"But I'm not depressed about going back to New York tomorrow. I'm looking forward to the work I have planned for next week."

His stunned expression told her what a powerful hold his fantasy had on him. Then he seemed to grasp for some explanation that wouldn't destroy it. "I can understand why you'd enjoy next week in New York. It's the Christmas season, and from what you did around here, I can see how much you love anything connected with the holidays. But once you get back to the regular grind, after New Year's, you'll see that—"

"It's not because of Christmas, Sam." She hated this, but leaving him with a fantasy that could never happen was even more cruel. "I've rediscovered the joy in my work. I hope to continue in interior design for a long, long time."

"But you said you were burned-out," he mumbled, looking dazed.

"Maybe I was. I've had lots of time to think in the

past few days, and I concluded that my burnout had more to do with my self-image than with the job. Eric had convinced me that my talents were pedestrian, especially compared to his. Then he left, handing me another blow. But I'm healing now." She stroked Sam's cheek and gazed at him, her heart full. "The country solitude, the weaving and most of all, your love, have given me new confidence. With that confidence all my old enthusiasm has come rushing back."

"But Anna, what about us?"

She winced at the agony threaded through his words. "I still love you, more every day," she said.

"I want us to be married," he said, the plea wrenching at her heart. "I want us to have children, to sit on the porch together, to be a *family*."

She smoothed the frown above the bridge of his nose, as if she could erase his tortured expression with a loving caress. "Families come in different shapes," she said gently. "I need to keep my job. It's a big part of what I am. Besides that, I've grown to like the hubbub of the city. If I couldn't be there a fair share of the time, I'd miss the excitement."

He turned away from her with a groan. "I can't believe you're saying this. What do you want, some sort of commuter marriage, where you rush home every weekend, get reacquainted with me and rush back on Sunday night?"

"You make it sound so grim," she said, putting her hand on his arm. "People find creative ways around these problems all the time. Lots of couples—"

"And what about the picture in your apartment? What about children?" he asked, still not looking at her. "Do you have a 'creative' solution for them, too? Or would you as soon skip that part, since it might be too complicated?"

"I don't know, Sam." She took her hand from his sleeve. "I don't have all the answers. In fact, I don't think it's up to me to provide them all. The idea in a partnership is for both people to work at a solution so each of them can have essentially what they want."

"I'll tell you what I want." He wheeled and looked at her with tears in his eyes. "I want a home, a real home, with you and me sharing the same bed every night. I want children who snuggle under their covers knowing that Mommy and Daddy are just down the hall if they wake up in the night with a bad dream. And I *don't* want the job of explaining to a sobbing three-year-old that his Mommy has gone off to the city again because she finds that life more exciting than staying with her family."

Anna gasped. "That is so rigid and traditional! It's a cozy picture for the man and the children, but where does it leave room for me to be myself?"

"What's wrong with the weaving?" he cried out. "Why can't you be yourself as a weaver?"

"Because I'm not your grandmother!"

He reeled back as if she'd slapped him. "I never said that I wanted you to—"

"Oh, yes you did." She clenched her fists at her sides. "Not directly, but in a million little ways, you've tried to reincarnate her in me. Well, I'll tell you something. Maybe Hilary Schute could be happy keeping house for her family, baking cookies, shopping for groceries, scrubbing floors and weaving in her spare time, but I can't. I have a career, and I intend to pursue it. If you can't accept that about me, we may as well part company now." Her heartbeat thundered in her ears while she waited for his answer. Surely he wouldn't let this issue tear them apart.

His shoulders sagged. "I see no way it would ever work out," he said. "We want two different things from life, Anna." His gaze, when he turned it on her, was bleaker than the gray sky outside the bedroom window. "You're right. I have been dreaming about recreating what my grandparents had. I still think it's a dream worth having."

"That's your answer, then?" she whispered, her eyes filling with tears.

"Yes." He turned away. "Yes, it is."

She struggled to breathe. It was over. Really over. "I'll...I'll arrange for your loom to be returned," she choked out.

"Don't bother." He cleared his throat. "I had intended to give it to you for Christmas. Consider it an early present."

"No."

"Anna, I don't want the loom back. It would only remind me of what we've lost."

"You didn't lose it! You threw it away!"

He faced her one last time. "I'm not the one with the career in the big city."

With a sob she turned and ran down the hall they'd stenciled together, past the poinsettias on the stairs, through the parlor filled with pine scent and the glow of ruby glass. She loved all of it, and she loved Sam, but not enough to sacrifice her freedom.

ANNA THREW HERSELF into her work that week. If this was to be her life, then she was determined to make the most of it. She'd planned several weaving projects to coordinate with designs she'd created for clients, and when she wasn't at the store or consulting in people's homes, she sat at the loom long into the night.

She'd decided to finish weaving everything that was already commissioned and then take a hiatus while she hunted around for a good buy on a used loom. She would have preferred returning Sam's loom immediately, but switching equipment at this stage might foul up some important weavings for her clients.

She worked through the weekend and tried to forget that Sam was back in Sumersbury by now. As she wove the skeins of yarn she'd bought from Tessie, she shoved aside several packages in shades of green. She'd intended to make a Christmas present for Sam, a blanket in the same weave as the blue one his grandmother had made. Only this blanket would be green to symbolize their love—evergreen, as the trees that Sam tended with such devotion.

Late each night just before she fell into a restless sleep, she'd wonder if the following day would bring a change of heart in Sam. She turned her answering machine on faithfully each day when she left for work, and each night she found only messages from clients who had become impatient trying to reach her at the store. Sam kept his silence.

Before her break with Sam, she'd expected to spend Christmas in Sumersbury. Now that was out, and she couldn't get a flight to her parents' this late. Typically, Vivian and Jimmy came through and invited Anna to spend the holiday weekend with them.

Anna promised to be at Vivian's house by noon on Sunday, Christmas Eve day. Vivian wanted Anna there by Saturday night, so they could all watch the Connecticut Christmas special on television together, but Anna declined. She had no desire to watch the special, and besides, she had plans for Saturday. She was returning Sam's loom.

Late Saturday morning, she picked up her rented van. Back at the apartment building, she offered a teenage boy ten dollars to help her carry and load the loom. Once that was accomplished, she tied it as securely as possible, but still it wobbled a little. No matter; she'd just drive slowly and carefully.

As she left the city and began the familiar drive to Sumersbury, she felt the same spirit of daring as when she'd set out on the path between her house and Sam's. The old Anna would have worried and fretted about how to transport the loom; the new Anna rented a van and delivered the goods.

She'd have to deal with Sam at the end of this journey, but her return of the loom would speak volumes. It was another way to tell him that she was in control of her life and didn't intend to relinquish that control to anyone, not even the man she loved. She didn't allow herself to dwell on what might have been, had Sam understood her needs. He'd made his position clear, and she would now underline hers.

Snowflakes spattered against the windshield, and she searched for the wiper mechanism. After blinking the headlights and squirting washer fluid over the window, she finally found the switch for the wipers. The snow added to her sense of adventure rather than frightening her. She knew the road, and once she'd delivered the loom, she'd head for her own farmhouse, where she'd stay until morning. The holiday weekend wasn't what she'd hoped for, but at least she was still in charge of her life.

JOHN HAD BEEN the foreman at Garrison's Christmas Tree Farm for years, long before Sam's grandparents died. Through all those years, he and Sam had been good friends, until now. Their differences began as soon as Sam returned from Washington.

The first day back, John called Sam on his short temper and demanded an explanation. Sam briefly outlined the scene with Anna and expected his

friend's support. John was big on family together-
ness, always had been.

To Sam's surprise, John took Anna's side and told
Sam his ideas were outdated. Sam responded by asking John to keep his opinions to himself. After that,
the two men didn't speak to each other except when
necessary.

John's comments plagued Sam during the days
and nights he was forced to live with the results of
Anna's design job on his house. He argued the subject
endlessly in his head, and his mood grew fouler still.

He considered staying home from Estelle's shindig
the Saturday night before Christmas. She'd rented a
large-screen television and was giving a party during
the Christmas special. Yet Sam knew that staying
home would hurt Estelle's feelings, and he couldn't
do that, either.

Around noon on Saturday, snow started falling,
and by two o'clock, it was heavy enough to discour-
age any last-minute customers from driving out for a
tree. Sam used the rest of the afternoon to balance the
books for a Hartford law firm, and by five he was on
the snowy, somewhat slippery, road to Estelle's.

ANNA SLOWED DOWN another five miles an hour.
Snow caked the windshield except for two fan-
shaped openings cleared by the wiper blades. She'd
turned on the van's headlights miles ago, and she
strained to make out the ruby taillights of the cars
creeping down the turnpike ahead of her. The proces-

sion of cars followed a snowplow like baby ducks trailing behind their mother.

Anna knew she'd be okay on the turnpike, even though a few times she'd felt her tires slip on the ice forming beneath the snow. But the plows couldn't keep up with all the exit and auxiliary roads, and she'd have to drive on them to reach Sumersbury.

It would be a picture-postcard Christmas there, she realized. The town had received two good snowfalls so far this year—one just in time for filming the special, and now this storm right before Christmas. She might have spent the most romantic holiday of her life in Sumersbury this weekend, if things had worked out differently with Sam. Anna tried to pull herself away from such thoughts, but the slow pace of the trip gave her too much time to think.

When the first signs for Sumersbury appeared on the turnpike, Anna was relieved. Her shoulders ached from gripping the steering wheel. The clock on the dash read almost five-twenty. No wonder she was tired. The trip had taken hours more than usual. She and Sam would have to unload the loom in the dark.

She took the exit road carefully. The van's steering indicated that ice was packed up inside the wheel wells. Anna knew the van had chains; the rental company had pointed them out to her. But she didn't relish the idea of getting out in this storm to put them on. She'd go slow. She'd make it.

Slowly she ground along the almost deserted roads. Treacherous though the weather was, it had created a holiday fairyland. Against the blanket of snow, multicolored holiday lights on trees and houses looked like gumdrops decorating a frosted gingerbread world. Chimneys smoked and windows glowed a friendly yellow in the darkness. Anna's heart wrenched. She wanted to be part of this landscape, too. Was she so wrong to want everything?

At last she reached the lane that led to Garrison's Christmas Tree Farm and her house, as well. She flipped on her turn signal to be safe, although there wasn't another vehicle in sight. The rock wall bordering the road wore a cap of snow at least a foot high, and the road hadn't been plowed. The faint tracks left by a car that had driven out of the lane were nearly obliterated by the addition of new snow. For the first time, she considered what she'd do if Sam wasn't home.

It was past six o'clock, she noticed, glancing at the lighted dashboard before she started the turn into the snowy lane. Well, if he wasn't home, she'd let herself in and write him a note. She could always drop the loom off early the next morning.

She hadn't turned left since leaving the main highway, and halfway into the lane, Anna realized the van wasn't responding well enough. The ice caked under the wheels gripped the tires with a terrible crunching sound, and the van skidded sideways. Fear washed over her, but she kept her foot off the brake and tried to steer in the direction of the skid. No good.

Anna saw the rock wall looming closer and wrenched at the wheel, but nothing happened. She was going to crash.

14

THE VAN SMACKED into the rock wall with a sickening thud that jerked Anna against her seat belt. She sat trembling, unconsciously trying to hold herself up straight although the van tilted crazily to the right. Snowflakes danced in the headlight beams, but the engine had stopped running when she hit the wall.

Willing her numbed fingers to work, she pried one hand loose from the steering wheel and turned the key in the ignition. The starter churned, but the engine wouldn't turn over. As the headlights began to flicker, she shut them off and eventually clicked the ignition key off, too. Even if she got the van started again, she'd never be able to drive out of the ditch and back onto the road without chains.

With the wipers shut down, the snow rapidly collected across her windshield and wrapped her in a white cocoon. In the silence, Anna had the crazy desire to curl up in her seat and go to sleep. Maybe if she slept, she'd wake up and discover this was a bad dream.

But it wasn't. Gradually, without the van's heater, cold started seeping in around the doors, and she remembered that the noise she'd heard when the van hit was of metal, certainly, but also of wood. With a sick sense of foreboding, she unhooked her seat belt and turned to look at Sam's loom.

THE CLINK OF TIRE CHAINS on the icy road reminded Sam of sleigh bells and made him wish that he still believed in Santa Claus. He could use a little wonder and magic in his life.

Not far from the turn into his lane, he noticed the van up against the rock wall and swore. He hoped nobody'd been hurt, because his was the nearest house, and they couldn't have gotten in unless they'd figured out where he hid his key.

From the snow piled up on the vehicle, Sam judged that the accident had taken place hours ago. He braked cautiously so as not to skid and add his truck to the disaster. Leaving the truck's engine running and the lights on, he stomped through the drifts and brushed snow away from the van's window. Nobody seemed to be inside. The door was locked when he tried it.

Returning to his truck, Sam decided to go home and call the highway patrol. He drove slowly and checked the sides of the lane for huddled figures or someone walking. Perhaps his house had afforded some shelter. The porch was better than nothing, he supposed.

By the time he pulled into his driveway, he knew they'd found his key. Smoke drifted from his chimney, and he certainly hadn't left a fire burning. Well,

he was glad they'd made themselves at home, who-
ever they were, although he wondered if he'd have
unexpected overnight guests. If they'd thought to use
his telephone, they'd surely have summoned help by
now. He hoped they hadn't taken off and left the fire
burning.

He parked the truck and headed for the porch. It
was snowing to beat the band. They probably
wouldn't get that van out of the ditch until after
Christmas. In the meantime, he'd try to help these
people locate somewhere else. He had some heavy-
duty thinking in mind for tonight, and he'd dearly
love to be alone to do it.

Inside the house, Anna heard the truck and then
Sam's boots on the porch. She got up from her spot on
the braided rug, where she'd sat in front of the fire,
her coat wrapped around her legs and feet and a
blanket from the upstairs hall closet around her
shoulders. She'd deliberately chosen a machine-
made blanket, not one woven by Sam's grandmother.

She faced the door like a prisoner lining up before
a firing squad. If she wanted the life of an independent woman, she had to take the consequences of her
actions. The coat crumpled to the floor as she stood,
but she held the blanket tight around her to stop her
hands from shaking.

Sam came through the door and stopped. "Anna!"

"You'd better close the door," she said quietly. "It's
very cold out there."

"It was you!" He threw the door shut and crossed

the room in three strides. "What happened? Are you hurt?"

"No, I'm not hurt."

"Are you sure?" He took her by the shoulders. "You look like you've been crying."

She stepped back, out of his reach. "Sam, I have something important to tell you."

"What's with the van? You're not moving out of your house, are you? Because I—"

"No, I'm not moving. Just let me talk for a minute. I drove the van here because I wanted to return the...the loom."

He frowned. "Anna, I told you that—"

"And I broke it when the van crashed," she said tonelessly. There. The news was out. She gripped the blanket tighter and waited for his reaction. Surely he'd be furious. She'd defied him by trying to bring it back in the first place, and then she'd imagined herself capable of returning it alone. As a result of her misguided confidence, she'd damaged something dear to him.

He gazed at her silently as the fire crackled beside them. She swallowed, knowing that whatever he might say she probably deserved. Even if the loom could be fixed, and she prayed that it could, offering to pay for repairs seemed inadequate. The loom would never be as strong or reliable again.

"Is that all?" he asked.

"I'd say that's quite enough." She watched the snow melt and glisten in his curly hair. He still had on his coat, and snow from his boots soaked into the braided rug. "I'll make no excuses about how this happened. I'm sorrier than I can say. Of course I'll try to have the loom fixed, but that doesn't make up for breaking it in the first place."

"You were crying. I know you were—your eyes are still red."

She glanced away. "Yes, I suppose I was."

"About the loom?"

She caught her lower lip in her teeth.

"Anna?"

"No, not just about the loom." She turned back to him, eyes brimming once more. "I didn't want to stay here until you got back. I wanted to walk on to my house, no matter how cold it was, no matter how snowy, so I could escape the memories here. But explaining about the loom in a note would have been cowardly, so here I am." She pressed her lips together to stop their trembling.

"You're no coward, Anna Tilford."

She sniffed and looked away again. She would have preferred harshness to the gentle expression on his face. If he'd be angry, she could be strong. Instead she saw compassion shining in his blue eyes, and that was hard to take. "Now that I've delivered my message, I'll go home," she said, taking the blanket from her shoulders and folding it.

"Think you'll follow the path tonight?"

She glanced up sharply. "Was that supposed to be funny?"

"No, but you are." He unbuttoned his coat. "What do you expect me to do—let you walk down a dark, snowy road at ten o'clock at night?"

She picked up her coat from the floor and put her arm in one sleeve. "How I get there isn't your problem."

"Anna," he said quietly, "I understand that you want to be your own person. You don't have to carry the thing to extremes."

She put her other arm into a sleeve. "I guess you're right. Would you please drive me home?"

"Sure." He tossed his coat over the back of a white leather armchair and nudged off his boots.

"Then why take off your coat and boots?"

"Because I'd like to tell you something first, if you're willing to listen." He walked over to the red patterned sofa and sat down. "Did you watch the special on television?"

"No." She'd forgotten that it had been on. She could have seen it, too, because she'd found the key and let herself into Sam's house well before seven. The accident and the damage to the loom had wiped all recollection of the special from her mind. "Why?" she finally thought to ask.

He patted the sofa next to him. "I sure wish you'd take that coat off and sit down. The room's pretty warm now, don't you think?"

She realized that he was right. The room had become warmer since he'd walked through the door. Or maybe the cold had left her once she'd confessed her misdeed. She couldn't think of any reason not to hear him out, either, so she took off her coat and walked over to the sofa.

He'd chosen one end; she chose the other. She curled her sock feet under her and faced him. "What about the special? You saw the show?"

"Estelle had a buffet dinner and invited a bunch of people to watch the special on a large-screen set she rented. I think she videotaped it, too, so you'll be able to see it sometime, if you like."

Anna shook her head. "No, thanks."

"You should take a look. You have a starring role."

"Me?"

"Throwing snow at the camera."

"Oh," She glanced toward the fire. "I figured they'd cut that."

"Well, they didn't. In fact, they showed most of that parade and edited out some of the house footage and some of the tree cutting—the two things they wanted when they planned the special. You know why they did that?"

"I can't imagine. I thought the whole idea was nostalgia, an old-fashioned country Christmas, not the circus atmosphere Estelle created."

Sam put his arm along the back of the couch, and his fingers rested inches from her shoulder. "That's what they thought they wanted, but Devlin, the guy who narrated the special, explained on camera that the fantasy didn't exist, despite everyone's valiant efforts to pretend that it did. Somewhere he learned that my house was professionally decorated."

"Oh, no! I certainly didn't tell."

"Of course you didn't, but Sumersbury is a small town, remember? Why would we imagine Dev wouldn't hear about your work if he stayed around for forty-eight hours?"

She couldn't help a small smile. "I guess you're right."

"Anyway, Dev also learned that we've never had Santa pulled through the streets of town by a pet deer dressed up like Rudolph, that the pond was created specifically for this occasion, and that even the town choir is a myth."

Anna groaned. "It must have been awful at Estelle's tonight. What did she say?"

"She was delighted! Because Dev, who is now her favorite actor of all time, praised the townspeople in general and Estelle in particular for good-naturedly trying to provide the nostalgia the network called for. The residents of Sumersbury became the heroes in the whole thing, and the network sheepishly admitted that what they'd envisioned hadn't existed for years."

"Amazing."

"I thought so."

She picked up a different, softer note in his words. She looked at him more carefully. "That's not all, is it?"

He shook his head. "John hasn't been too friendly with me lately."

"John?"

"You see, John thinks I'm a lot like the television network, looking for something that doesn't exist anymore."

She sat quietly, but her heart began pounding faster.

"I told him to get lost with his theories, but I haven't been able to forget what he said, especially after I watched the special tonight."

She was afraid to move, afraid that what was happening wouldn't be true. And she wanted desperately for it to be true.

"We all laughed and groaned as the skaters tumbled into each other," he continued, "and then suddenly there you were, larger than life on that big screen and flinging snow at the camera. I loved you so much at that moment that it hurt. It still does."

"Oh, Sam. I love you, too." Her eyes filled with tears again.

"I was wrong, Anna. I once thought of you as some modern-day version of my grandmother. But tonight on that screen, I saw just you, the woman I love. If you'll—if you'll forgive me, I'd like to start over with that proposal. I'd like to talk about some of those alternatives you mentioned."

She left her end of the couch and flung herself into his arms with such force that she partially knocked the breath from him.

"Is that a yes?" he said, coughing and laughing at the same time.

"Most definitely." She cuddled against him and smiled into his face. "Maybe this Christmas can be salvaged, after all."

He held her tight and peppered her face with kisses. "I thought I'd have to say all this over the phone or drive to New York and slip notes under your door. Can you stay? Can you spend Christmas with me?"

"I'll have to call Vivian, but yes, I can stay. Besides, I don't have anything drivable to take me back." Her joy dimmed. "Sam, I'm really upset about the loom."

"I think it's a good thing. I was too reverential about that loom, about everything connected with my grandparents' life. All that's happened only reminds me that you and our relationship is all that matters. The rest is old-fashioned drivel."

"Now, Sam, let's not go overboard," she protested, laughing at his vehemence. "Some old-fashioned customs and ideas are wonderful. I still want to weave, and I've loved adding all the simple country touches to this house and putting up the trees and using your family decorations on the big one here in the parlor." She remembered something else. "Sam, I don't have a present for you."

He scooped her up in his arms and stood. "That's what you think. There's one old-fashioned custom I never intend to give up."

"What's that?" she asked, guessing by the direction he was headed.

"Late-night sleigh rides," he murmured, nestling his cheek against hers as he carried her up the stairs.

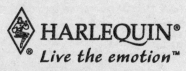

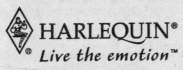

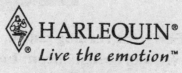